TEMPTING TARGET

Savannah Stuart

Cover art: Jaycee of Sweet 'N Spicy Designs
Author website: http://www.savannahstuartauthor.com

Tempting Target was originally published in 2008 as *City of Secrets* by Katie Reus and in 2011 under its current title by a different publisher. It has been slightly revised, updated, and edited from its original version.

Tempting Target/Savannah Stuart. – 2nd ed.
ISBN-13: 978-1502467584
ISBN-10: 1502467585
eBook ISBN: 9780996087452

For Kari Walker. I think it's possible you love David more than I loved creating him. Thank you for your constant support.

Praise for the books of Savannah Stuart

"Fans of sexy paranormal romance should definitely treat themselves to this sexy & fun story." —Nina's Literary Escape

"I enjoyed this installment so much I'll be picking up book one...worth the price for the punch of plot and heat."
—Jessie, HEA USA Today blog

"...a scorching hot read." —The Jeep Diva

"This story was a fantastic summer read!" —Book Lovin' Mamas

"If you're looking for a hot, sweet read, be sure not to miss Tempting Alibi. It's one I know I'll revisit again and again."
—Happily Ever After Reviews

"You will not regret reading the previous story or this one. I would recommend it to anyone who loves a great shifter story."
—The Long & Short of It (Power Unleashed)

"...a fun and sexy shapeshifter book and definitely worth the read."
—The Book Binge

CHAPTER ONE

Jade Hadley perched on the edge of her butterfly stool as she stared out the window of *My Sister's Closet*, her clothing boutique. The scene in front of her was familiar and one she saw every day. A miniature potted palm tree used to prop open the French door swayed silently with the chilly breeze, and the sea of tourists so prevalent during the day had thinned to a trickle on the street.

Shadows and blurred shapes only danced in front of her line of sight because she couldn't seem to focus on anything lately.

Anything other than her hideous lack of sex.

It had been two years since she'd seen a naked man. Two years since she'd pressed her bare body up against another one. Two. Freaking. Years.

Until recently, she hadn't cared. Immediately after her husband's death, getting out of bed and showering had been her biggest accomplishment. Hoorah for her.

For the most part, she loved her life the way it was, but lately it seemed everywhere she looked, she saw couples. Couples holding hands. Couples on dates. Couples renting videos together. They all looked so annoyingly happy.

Sighing, she stood and quickly closed down her shop. A blast of fresh sea air rolled over her as she stepped onto the cobblestones of St. George Street. Rows of shops blocked her view, but she could always smell the ocean. That moist sea air was something one couldn't escape living so near the coast. Her store was in the middle of Saint Augustine's historic downtown district, and she lived almost exactly a mile and a half away.

The walk home was quick and the moment she stepped through her front door, the phone started ringing. She grabbed it on the fourth ring, just before her answering machine picked up. "Hello?"

"Hey little sister, you sound like you've been out running." Maya, her older sister's familiar voice greeted her.

She snorted. "Not this late. I just got home."

"Well, that wouldn't be a problem if you weren't the only freak left on the planet without a cell phone, now would it? Seriously, who has a land line anymore?" Sarcasm laced her voice.

"Please spare me, I get that enough from Mom. And I do have one." Well she had, but her trusty flip phone had finally died and now she needed to replace it. She'd cancelled her service since her contract had been up anyway. The only problem was, she couldn't find anything that didn't have a hundred apps she'd never use. Or as durable as her old phone. That thing had taken a beating. Besides, she worked enough and had a tablet and laptop so she could check e-mails or whatever else for her business. She hated the idea of being connected online 24/7. "I was actually going to call you and see if we could get together this week for lunch." She shrugged out of her green pea coat and pulled out a bottle of Pinot Noir.

"Good because I've needed someone to vent to," Maya grumbled.

"Uh, oh. This doesn't sound good. I'm guessing my darling little nephews got into something they shouldn't have. Again." Brian and Owen were three-year-old twin terrors with a knack for doing exactly as they pleased and begging forgiveness later.

"You guessed right. I still don't know how it happened. They were both eating peanut butter and jelly sandwiches at the kitchen table. In the amount of time it took me to transfer a clean load of clothes into the dryer and start another load, they'd made a mural on my new love seat."

"What did they use?" Inwardly she cringed, already knowing the answer.

"What else? Peanut butter and jelly. I'm assuming because it was available." Her sister let out a resigned sigh.

Jade resisted the urge to laugh. When they were kids, they'd done much worse.

"Aren't you going to say anything?" Though muted, annoyance was still very evident in Maya's voice.

She choked back a laugh. "I don't even know *what* to say."

"Saying nothing is better than saying something stupid."

Uh-oh. "What did Colin say?"

"He said 'boys will be boys'. He's so casual about it, but if they'd done something to his precious truck or huge flat-screen, I'm sure he'd have had a lot more to say than that. I made him sleep on the couch."

"I'm sure that lasted all of ten minutes."

"You might be surprised," Maya muttered.

Jade frowned at her sister's words. Married for four years, Maya and Colin still acted like newlyweds. Occasionally, when she looked at the two of them so happy together she ached. Her sister's tone was unusual. "What's going on with you two?"

"We... never mind."

"What is it?"

"Seriously. It's nothing."

Jade bit her tongue but she hated that Maya didn't open up to her. And Jade knew why. Just because she was a widow Maya seemed to think she couldn't vent about her husband because she had one. She understood her sister wanted to protect her feelings but she missed the way they used to talk. Now wasn't the time to grill her about it though.

"All right, that's enough out of me. What have I missed in the past day?"

Jade slipped off her boots and sat on one of the high top swivel chairs. "I've come to a decision, but I need your help. I want..." For weeks she'd struggled to think of an appropriate way to say, 'It's been so long since I've had sex that I'm wondering if they've changed it.'

Her sister would understand. That wasn't what worried her. Saying the words aloud meant she was truly moving on. She didn't want to betray Aidan's memory, but she missed that physical connection. At the same time, the thought of letting another man touch her scared the holy hell out of her.

"I don't have time to play twenty questions. Out with it," Maya prodded in her familiar big sister tone.

"I'm ready to start dating again. Soon. It's been too long since I've seen a naked man. I'm in need of some seriously hot sex. Or just some regular sex. And I want an orgasm that does *not* include a battery operated machine. I'm tired of living like a nun." The words tumbled out once she got started.

Maya exhaled loudly. "You scared the crap out of me, Jade. I thought it was something serious."

"This *is* serious." She frowned at her sister's blasé response.

"Sweetie, Mom and I have been waiting the past few months for you to say this."

"What?"

"Yep. Mom and I have a whole fleet of men dying to take you out. Well, maybe not that many, but we definitely have some in mind. But if I were you, I'd stick with the men I pick, not Mom. You know how she can get—"

"Why didn't you say something sooner?"

"We were waiting until you were ready. It wouldn't have mattered how many great guys we had lined up if it wasn't the right time for you."

She started to protest, but the truth of her sister's words hit her with startling accuracy. If they had tried to set her up with anyone, even three months ago, she would have most definitely said no. "It's going to be weird dating again. Where am I even going to meet anyone?"

She wasn't really into the bar scene. Even before Aidan, she hadn't been. Compared to her former party girl sister, she'd always preferred to go boating or hit the beach in lieu of staying out all night drinking. Occasionally she went out for drinks with girlfriends after work but was almost always home by nine.

"You just leave that up to Mom and me. In fact, I think I have the perfect candidate for you. There's this man, Rick, that Colin's been working with for the past year who would be a *perfect* first date for you."

"No, no cops." Maya's husband was a detective in Saint Augustine so naturally all of his friends were in law enforcement. "And no firefighters either. I don't want anyone with a dangerous job. I want someone with a normal nine to five who comes home for dinners."

"Jade, you can't limit yourself like—"

"Yeah, I really can." After being married to a US Marshal, who'd left at all hours of the night, her worry had been endless. She wasn't putting herself through that again.

"Fine, but this isn't over. What about David?"

"I haven't talked to him about it yet. I figured I'd wait until he got back in town. Hopefully he'll be home this weekend. I haven't seen him in a couple weeks, so he's due back any day." Every time she called him it went straight to voicemail so she assumed he was out of the country. Last time they'd gotten together he'd said something about a security job, but it was hard to keep his schedule straight. It was only Monday, so she knew not to expect him back until at least Friday or Saturday.

"*No.*" Her sister stressed the word. "I mean what about dating David?"

Jade's hand jerked slightly, spilling wine on the granite counter. "Are you out of your mind? He was Aidan's best friend. What's the matter with you?"

"I think he'd be good for you, and so does Mom." Her sister's words echoed in her brain and bounced around for all of two seconds before she dismissed them.

Completely.

She still remembered the sorrow in David's dark eyes the day he'd come to her with the news of Aidan's death. He hadn't had to say a word; she'd known the second he'd shown up on her doorstep. That was the first time she'd ever seen a man cry—really cry—and to see a man that tough break down, she'd known only one thing could have happened.

"What? He's not good looking enough?" Maya asked, and Jade could practically see the smirk on her sister's face.

David was a wonderful friend, but she didn't consider him boyfriend or husband material. It's not that he wasn't attractive. Even she couldn't deny that. If it wasn't for his nose, which had been broken more than once, he'd almost be too good looking. His features were sharp, Slavic in appearance. With a square jaw, sharp cheekbones, and deep charcoal eyes the man had to know he looked good. He stood close to six foot three, and no matter how often he shaved, he seemed to have a permanent five o'clock shadow. His thick black hair always hung a little too long on the sides, and his eyes rarely revealed glimpses into what he was thinking.

They might be friends but he was a very private person, even with her. Not to mention he had a primitive side to him that sometimes put her on edge. He'd never done anything outright to make her wary, and in reality, he'd been one of the best friends she could ask for. Still, she knew it was there just the same, lurking beneath the surface.

And there was no way she was discussing *any* of that was her sister. "Be serious, Maya." She grabbed a rag and started to clean up the crimson mess she'd made.

"Fine, fine. I have some candidates in mind but I want to narrow down my list first. Oh, and one more thing." There was a long pause on Maya's end. Jade heard a crash in the background. Surprisingly Maya stayed on the line. "You need to take off your ring."

A lump settled in her throat. She still hadn't taken off her wedding ring. It wasn't as if she hadn't considered it, but every time the thought crossed her mind, guilt engulfed her. Her first instinct was to argue, but she knew her sister was right. "I know."

After they disconnected, Jade trudged up the stairs to her room. The house was eerily quiet. Safely in her room, she sat on the edge of the bed and stared at her left hand. It was now or never. She slipped the plain, platinum wedding band off her ring finger and placed it in the middle of her chestnut dresser. Minutes passed, but she didn't move. She was rooted to the spot, mesmerized by the ring, almost afraid to take her eyes away from it.

It's time to let go. Aidan's voice sounded in her head as clear as if he were in the same room. A strange sensation filled her. One she hadn't felt in quite some time. Relief. The vise that had gripped her heart for so long, loosened. It didn't completely release, but it was a start. With care, she placed the ring in her handcrafted mahogany jewelry box and clicked the lock into place.

"It's time." Though no one was around to hear, saying the words aloud gave her an unexpected sense of peace.

CHAPTER TWO

David McIntyre leaned back in the leather seat of
the luxurious twin engine jet as the nose of the
plane dropped and they skidded onto the runway. He
grabbed his carry-on from the seat next to him, made his
way to the front, and waited for the pilots to open the
hatch. His return flight from the Caribbean had been as
uneventful as the recent security job. The rest of the
security team had all flown back to their respective cities
but the band that hired him had flown him home on one
of their private jets. The small but impressive plane sat
twelve comfortably, but with the exception of the pilot
and co-pilot, he was alone.

Despite his crazy schedule, he was grateful for his
success. Two years ago, when his best friend died, he'd
quit his job as a US Marshal and started his own security
company. The thought of working the same job without
Aidan by his side had made him feel...hollow. He'd
gained enough contacts from his many years in the Navy, and then from working as a US Marshal, that jobs
had literally fallen into his lap. If only his personal life
was as smooth as his professional one.

A few minutes later, he thanked the pilot and descended the stairs leading to the tarmac. Without waiting another moment, he got into the idling taxi. The best perk about having an official passport was that he didn't have to wait around for his luggage or deal with security checks. The driver half turned in his seat and asked him where he wanted to go. Without thinking, David rattled off Jade's address. He inwardly cursed, but he also didn't correct himself. It was bad for him to see her too often, but he did it nonetheless. Every time he came home, he had to see her.

She was his addiction. His secret addiction.

Weeks had passed since he'd seen her last. Fifteen days to be exact, but who was counting? The need to be near her sometimes overwhelmed him. For three years he'd been trying to get over her but to no avail. Apparently, he was a masochist.

He shut his eyes, trying to block out the mental image of her but that only made it worse. Her skin was always a golden brown, and she usually left her long, honey-caramel colored hair down, swinging seductively around her shoulders. Her emerald eyes always seemed to be filled with laughter. A man could lose himself forever in those deep, exotic pools. And forget about her curves. His whole body flared to life just thinking about them. He never understood why she hated her hips. More times than he cared to admit, he'd fantasized about what it would feel like to wrap his hands around them as she rode him. Or as he took her from behind.

Of course, she had no clue how he felt. No one did. He'd heard about love at first sight, but he'd never bought into that bullshit. Until he met her. At first, he convinced himself it was lust, and that it would pass. He wished every day that lust was all he felt. Lust he could get over. Lust would mean he only wanted her physically. Unfortunately, his feelings strengthened each time they were together. Over the years, it had become easier to hide them.

For the first and only year of her marriage, he'd screwed every woman he could in an effort to get her out of his system. That hadn't worked. After Aidan died, he'd stopped sleeping around all together. She might not exactly be on the market, but with Jade single, no other woman had a chance.

The jostling of the car over the old bricks and cobblestones brought him back to reality. He'd been so lost in his thoughts he didn't realize how close they were to her place. He glanced out the window to find the sky now dark, save for a few street lights and the pale moon. The cab driver turned down the familiar palm tree-lined street and jerked to a halt in front of her two story Mediterranean-style house.

David's heart pounded erratically in his chest. It was nearly eight, so he knew she'd be home from work, even if she'd walked. Which she probably had.

He handed the cab driver a fifty and told him to keep the change. After wiping his sweaty palms on his jeans, he grabbed his small carry-on and then his larger bag from the trunk. Mentally, he tried to prepare himself for seeing her again. It was a fruitless effort. Adrenaline tore through his body like heat lighting flashing across the sky at the thought of her.

He stepped through the stucco archway, knocked once on the russet colored door, and forced himself to breathe. A few seconds later, the door swung open. Jade greeted him in bare feet, a worn out pair of boxers two sizes too big for her, and one of his old football jerseys that looked absolutely ridiculous on her petite frame. He must have left it at her place. Something primal inside him smiled at seeing her in his clothes. His heart slammed against his ribcage when a bright smile spread across her face. A tropical scent teased his nose. She always wore the same intoxicating aroma. He could never quite figure out what the combination was. Coconut, jasmine, and something else designed to drive him crazy.

She threw her body against his in a staggering hug. Luckily, he was prepared for it. That was another thing he loved about her, she didn't do anything half ass.

When she hugged someone, she put her whole body into it.

"I take it you missed me." He held onto her as long as was socially acceptable and fought the hard-on he got every time she touched him. He forced himself to ignore what the press of her soft breasts against his chest did to him.

"Of course I did. But more importantly, where's my present?" She grinned as she stepped out of his embrace.

"Is that all you care about? Presents?" He lifted his eyebrows, feigning insult.

"You know you're the only man in my life. I have to take advantage." She grabbed his hand and dragged him into the circular entryway, shutting the heavy door behind her with a loud bang.

His next words died on his lips. It was a flippant comment. He knew that. In spite of what his head told him, to hear her say he was the only man in her life, sped his heart rate up. Considerably.

"I can't believe you didn't call me first."

In an effort to keep up with her dizzying pace, he dropped both his bags. A dull echo sounded against the ceramic tile. He just shrugged and grinned. "I saw the time and knew you'd be walking home when I called. Besides, it's not as if you've replaced your cell phone yet."

"You sound like Maya. I swear, sometimes I think the two of you conspire together." Jade rolled her eyes and led him into her kitchen.

He followed, inhaling the fresh fragrance that trailed behind her. The walk from the foyer down the open hallway to the kitchen was a long established one. Whenever he visited, they talked in the kitchen for at least an hour until she eventually moved them into her living room. It was almost like a tradition. He didn't have much stability in his life, and in a way, her little traditions kept him grounded. Made him feel like part of a family.

While she busied herself at the refrigerator, he shrugged out of his brown leather jacket and took a seat at the granite island cook top.

"I've got water, sweet tea, and milk. Unless you need something stronger?" She peered into the stainless steel refrigerator then threw him a backward glance.

Being a southerner, it was in his blood to drink sweet tea, but after a long flight he always craved a beer. "A beer would be great if you have any." She handed him a Heineken and pulled out a bottle of white wine.

"The kitchen looks great," he said, taking in his sur-roundings with appreciation. The last time he'd been there, dust, plastic wrap, and old wooden planks had been strewn everywhere.

She didn't turn around from opening her wine bottle but nodded in affirmation. "Tell me about it. It's hard to believe those jerks finally finished. I don't know what got into them, but they finally got their act together and actually started working. I swear, if I heard the words 'we'll be done next week' one more time I was going to lose my mind."

David smothered a smile. He didn't tell her, but he'd had a private meeting with the contractors she'd hired. The job should have taken a month at the most. Three months later, they were still making empty promises. She'd been too lax about it, so he'd taken matters into his own hands. Now the kitchen boasted tumbled marble floors, rope lighting above the cabinets, a new copper sink, and vintage pendant lamps that hung above the center island. He didn't know shit about style but it fit her.

David sat back and drank in the sight of her as she pulled a wine glass down from one of the open shelves. When she stretched up, her calf muscles flexed and his cock jerked to attention. He really was twisted. An eyeful of her calves and he was ready to take her against the kitchen counter.

He frowned when she poured herself a small amount. "Not even a full glass? Is that a hint you don't want me here?"

She grinned and swatted his shoulder as she took a seat next to him. "No, I have a date in less than an hour, and I don't want to get sloshed before it's even started. Can you imagine? My first date in years, and I get carried home. You know what a lightweight I am." She let out a silvery laugh that pierced his heart.

Blood roared in his ears. After the word 'date', everything else funneled out. Liquid fire slowly and deliberately lapped across his chest. He took a swig of his beer and stared blindly at the ceiling. Dating? She was *dating*? He'd seen her two weeks ago and she hadn't mentioned anything. She might as well have said she'd joined a terrorist organization in his absence.

Then he noticed something different. He'd known something was off when she'd opened the door, but she'd been moving around so fast he hadn't been able to place it. She wasn't wearing her wedding ring anymore. Somehow he found his voice, but the words stuck in his throat. "When did you start dating again?"

She wrinkled her nose as if to make fun, then pain flashed in her eyes, and her voice came out soft. "This is my first one since...this is the first one since you know. I would have talked to you about it, but I couldn't get a hold of you and I didn't want to leave a message on your voicemail."

"So who is he?" *Damn it*, he inwardly cursed. He didn't need details.

A blush crept across her high, exotic cheekbones. "I haven't actually met him yet. His name is William. Apparently my mom knows him from church."

William. What a dumb fucking name. Probably some pansy ass preppy. He forced a tight smile then stared down into his beer. No matter how wide he stretched his mouth, the smile wouldn't reach his eyes, and she would see it. With one final swig, he finished his drink and stood up. Despite the cool atmosphere, his body was a raging inferno. His lungs refused to expand, and something comparable to a knife twisted in his gut. Getting out of this room was suddenly the most important thing in the world. "I can clear out of here if you need to get ready."

She gently touched his arm and pushed him back down. "Please stay. I'll only be gone an hour or two at the most. It's been too long since I've seen you. Besides, I'm sure you have laundry you need to do, and I know your dryer is still broken. If you want, you can take care of it while I'm gone, and stay until I get home?"

The truth was that he'd purchased a new top of the line washer and dryer over six months ago. He just hadn't gotten around to saying anything about it to her. Sometimes he wanted an excuse to come over.

He wanted to tell her no, that he should get home, but morbid curiosity won over. "Sure, I'll stick around." It couldn't hurt to know the competition.

Jade's face lit up and the knife inside him twisted deeper. "Great, now if you don't mind, I do need to finish getting ready, because I don't think this is suitable attire. As soon as I'm home, we're getting caught up." She placed her empty wine glass in the sink and left him sitting at the island.

"Fuck that," he said to the empty room. If she was moving on, he was going to make damn sure she moved on with him. He was through being patient. She didn't know it yet, but she belonged to him.

* * *

Discreetly as she could, Jade glanced at the slim, silver watch on her arm that looked more like a bangle than a timepiece. Then she looked out the window of her date's new BMW—the only reason she was aware it was new was because he'd told her. Twice.

Palm trees and historic houses flew by at a normal speed, but she couldn't stop herself from counting down the seconds until he pulled into her driveway. The moment the car jerked to a halt, her hand was already on the handle.

"Well, thanks for a great evening," she said, and hoped annoyance didn't show on her face.

"I could come in for a drink—"

"No, I have to get up early for work, but maybe I'll see you later." Clutch purse in one hand, shawl in the other, she jumped out of the car and tried to walk as quickly as she could without looking like she was making a mad dash for her house. Safely inside, she locked the door, sagged against it, and rubbed her temple.

"That bad huh?" David's voice startled her.

She looked up to find him staring at her with barely concealed amusement. The overhead light in the foyer was dimly lit, but a pale moonbeam shone through the high-windowed archways, perfectly illuminating David's form. It took a moment for her eyes to focus, and when they did, she realized he wasn't wearing a shirt.

Her breath caught in her throat. All coherent thought left her brain at the sight of his muscular, bare chest, and long, lean form. Good Lord, the man looked like he was cut from stone.

Despite her desire not to look, her eyes trailed the length of his body, complete with a ripped eight pack— who the hell had an eight pack anyway. He didn't have much hair, but there was a light line that trailed below his belt line. She stopped directly at his belt when a sudden vision of what was *beneath* those pants filled her mind. Everything about him was big and she just knew he'd be well-endowed.

Not that she cared. *She didn't.* So why did a sudden rush of heat find its way between her legs? And why the hell had she even let her thoughts stray in this direction? This was *David*. He was her friend. This was her sister's fault for even mentioning him as a possible dating candidate.

A spicy, masculine scent tickled her nose. It must be his aftershave. Strange that she'd never noticed how good he smelled before. She swallowed hard. "What, uh…" She was blatantly staring but couldn't seem to drag her eyes away from all that taut skin. She also couldn't seem to formulate another word after 'uh'.

He glanced down and smacked his washboard stomach the way men who know they look good do. "Sorry, I didn't think you'd be back so soon, and I threw the shirt I was wearing in with the rest of my laundry."

Cargo pants hung from his trim waist. Jade fought the heat rushing to her cheeks and forced herself to focus on his face. "No, that's okay, I just didn't expect you to be…" She thought of saying half naked, but the thought of him naked brought even more heat to her already burning cheeks, so she finished with, "…partially clothed."

"My clothes should be done by now, I'll be back in a second." He turned and disappeared down the hallway.

Before she could tell him not to worry about it, his broad shoulders and very sculpted backside had disappeared around the corner. It was probably a good thing he was putting clothes on because apparently she had a problem focusing around half naked men. Maybe she wasn't ready for a hot affair after all. The mere sight of naked flesh and she turned into a stammering idiot. A minute later, he was back, and she could almost swear he looked triumphant. About what though, she couldn't imagine.

"So, how was the date?" His question interrupted her scrutiny of his face.

She let out an overdramatic sigh. "Horrible. Well, maybe not horrible, but it wasn't good. I hate that I wasted such a great dress on that guy." Despite the chill in the air, she'd opted to wear a sleek, emerald formfitting dress. It was one of her 'go to' dresses when she needed a boost of confidence because it matched her eyes and made her butt look great. She slipped her three-inch sling backs off and followed him into her living room. She moved a stack of magazines off the big couch and into the rattan magazine rack so David could sit.

He always chose the bigger couch to stretch out on, although he somehow still seemed too large for it. Once he sat, she moved to the smaller love seat across from him. An undersized bamboo coffee table separated them, and for some reason she was glad to have that little barrier.

She tucked her feet under her legs and tried to get the vision of his half naked, perfectly sculpted body out of her mind. Racking her brain, she tried to remember a time when she'd ever seen him without his shirt off but couldn't recall a single one. No, she definitely would have remembered the distinctive scar that ran half the length of his chest. He looked so calm and relaxed sitting across from her that she was embarrassed that she kept thinking about all that exposed skin.

"All right, tell me about it." A small grin played across his face.

"The first words out of his mouth when we sat down at the restaurant were, 'I hate to admit this, but I forgot my wallet'."

David's dark eyes narrowed into slits. "Are you kidding me? Tell me you didn't pay."

She shook her head and smothered a grin. "I wish I was, and no, I did not. I told him we better leave then because I didn't have any cash with me." She gestured to the impossibly tiny, satin clutch purse next to her.

"Are you telling me that you left the house without any money? What if you'd been stranded somewhere?" he practically growled.

"Of course I didn't, I always carry my check card with me. I just didn't tell him that. After all, he's the one who called me up and invited me out."

He leaned back against the couch, but she could still see the tension humming through his body. "What did he do?"

"I watched him squirm for a minute until he miraculously remembered that he had a credit card for emergencies in his car." She rolled her eyes. "This guy really was a piece of work."

"Did things improve?"

"Not really. The only positive thing to come out of the night is that we went to La Pentola. Still, I couldn't decide if I wanted to stuff breadsticks in my ears or in *his mouth* just to shut him up. He didn't open *any* of my doors and he talked about what a psycho his ex-girlfriend was the entire time. No, I take that back, there was a brief reprieve near the end of the date. Somehow the topic of eminent domain got brought up, and when I offered my opinion I got a ten point lecture about why I was wrong. I swear, if he'd brought his laptop, I think he'd have probably given me a Power Point presentation." She shuddered. "I didn't think I'd been out of the game that long. Honestly, am I expecting too much?"

He shook his head slightly. "No, you're not. That jackass is lucky you even agreed to go out with him.

She smiled at his darkened expression. It was nice not to feel like her expectations were crazy.

"What are you doing going out on a blind date in the first place? I wouldn't think *you* would have any trouble meeting eligible men." David looked at her with such incredulousness she felt a little embarrassed.

She shrugged and tried to ignore the heat that rushed to her cheeks. "I don't really know where I'd go to meet men anymore. Most of my friends are married, and I'm not into the bar scene. Even if I was, I don't have anyone to go with me anymore. It's not as if I meet any eligible men at work. The men who come into my store are either shopping for their girlfriends or wives—or they're gay. That leaves being set up. I just can't believe my mother, who I'm never trusting again, thought I would be interested in that guy."

Wanting to change the subject, she turned the focus back on him. "So what about you? How many crazy girl-friends are you entertaining this week?" She resisted the urge to smile. The last woman he'd quasi-dated had named both of her breasts, and apparently had no problem informing him on their first date—and anyone within a ten mile radius—of their size, likes, and dislikes.

"None." He raked a hand through his unruly hair, and his jaw and neck visibly tensed.

"Seriously? Or you just don't want to talk about it?" Normally, she left it alone if he didn't want to talk about his dates, but he hadn't brought anyone up in a long time and lately she'd been wondering why.

He cleared his throat, but he finally answered. "I haven't dated anyone in a while, Jade."

"Oh, I'd just assumed." Before Aidan died, David had brought bimbo after bimbo to all of their cook-outs or double dates, and it was never the same woman twice. And each one was dumber than the next. Back then she hadn't known him that well but his dating choices had always surprised her.

"I...It's hard to date with my schedule." He sighed and rubbed a hand across his unshaven face. She was under the impression that he wanted to say more, but something in his dark eyes told her not to push.

"I'm sure it is." Relief spread through her body like wildfire, though she wasn't sure why. Whatever strange apprehension she'd experienced disappeared, and she was able to relax. For the next hour, they caught up on the past two weeks in each other's lives.

The look on David's face after her last story was priceless. "They did *what* to their neighbor's car?"

Jade nodded. "You heard me right. They saw the neighbor's dog do it and decided it must be all right. Maya had put them in her van to take them over to Mom and Dad's. She ran in the house to grab her purse and by the time she'd returned, they'd escaped. She found them with their pants around their ankles spraying the tires of the Sanchez's brand new Mercedes. With Mrs. Sanchez in the driver's seat."

David let out a whoop of laughter and shook his head. "I don't know how your sister does it. What a handful."

"They're worth it." She couldn't hide the wistful note in her voice.

His face softened. "Kids? Is that why you've decided to start dating again?"

"I guess I just want the option. I don't think Aidan would have wanted me to be single the rest of my life?" She didn't mean to, but the last part came out as a question. For some reason she felt she needed David's approval. He'd been like family to Aidan, and she cared about his opinion more than she'd ever admit to anyone.

David stared at her for so long she thought he wasn't going to answer, but finally, he spoke. "No, I know he wouldn't have."

"Do you ever think about him?"

His neck muscles tightened. "All the time."

"Me too. Maybe not as much anymore, though."

At his raised eyebrows she shook her head. "I just mean that I really am ready to move on. It's not like it happened overnight, but I finally feel peace about my decision."

"Good. He would have wanted you happy more than anything. I remember the day he called me up and told me he was getting married. At first I thought he was messing with me. But when I met you I understood why he was giving up bachelorhood."

She snorted. "Ha ha."

"Why is that funny?" His dark eyes narrowed a fraction as if he were seriously offended.

She knew better. "Come on. If I remember correctly, you couldn't stand me."

"What?" He shifted uncomfortably in his seat.

"Oh please. The week before our wedding you barely talked to me. Aidan told me you'd eventually come around but that in a way I was stealing your best friend."

"He said that?"

She started to respond, but a yawn escaped instead.

David chuckled and pushed up from the couch. He pulled her to her feet. "I can take a hint. Do you mind driving me home before you fall asleep? I took a taxi here."

"Why don't you just stay?"

David went very still. "What?"

She shrugged, unsure what the big deal was. He'd stayed over before. "Just sleep in the guest room, and I'll take you home in the morning before work. It's supposed to rain tomorrow anyway, so I'll probably drive instead of walk."

"It never rains in February." His eyes narrowed slightly, and she knew he wasn't buying it.

"I know. I'm too tired to drive, and since tomorrow's Saturday I can sneak in a little late. Do you mind staying here, or do you really want to sleep in your own bed tonight? If you do I understand."

He'd been on the go for the past few weeks, and it would be understandable if he wanted to go home, but she hoped he said no. That last glass of wine had kicked in and sandbags weighed her eyelids down. He didn't live far, but for how she felt, it was far enough.

"No, I'll stay here. I don't want you driving alone at night or with even a hint of alcohol in your system. As payment you can cook me breakfast in the morning *and* have dinner with me on Sunday. To make up for your bad date."

She laughed and trudged up the stairs, forcing herself to stay awake just a few minutes longer. "Deal. I can make you eggs, bacon, and grits tomorrow. How's that sound?" She threw a quick glance over her shoulder only to catch him blatantly staring at her butt in more than typical male admiration. She'd seen that look from men before, many times, but never from David. Never, *ever* from him.

She whipped back around and tripped over her own feet in the process. His hands snaked out and gripped her waist in an almost intimate embrace. No, not almost. It was definitely intimate. Or maybe she just wanted it to be. *Where had that thought come from?*

A jolt of awareness surged through her body hot and fast. It had been a long time since a man had held her. He was just steadying her, but the sudden responsive-ness she experienced was overpowering. His hands simply lingered around her waist when an unexpected image of what it would feel like to have his hands holding her breasts popped into her mind. The feel of his large, callused hands teasing her would be amazing. She just knew it. For such a big guy he was always so gentle with her. She could just imagine one of those big hands cupping her mound while he—She went rigid at the thought.

What was the matter with her?

He must have sensed her discomfort because his hands immediately dropped. Instead of removing them completely, he placed a protective hand on the small of her back. Tingles shot up her spine, and a strange feminine flutter danced in her stomach.

"You all right?" The pressure from his hand increased slightly.

She nodded but didn't turn around, afraid of what she'd see on his face if she did. "I'm fine, I guess I'm just a little more tired than I realized."

Even though he didn't need directions, she led him to the guest room and pulled out some towels in case he wanted to shower.

"It'll get better, you know." His voice was soft and comforting.

"What will?" A little confused, she looked up at him and suddenly felt very small. Without her heels on, he towered over her. Not to mention, the temperature in the room had suddenly risen about a thousand degrees. What was that about?

"Moving on. It'll get easier with time. You've already taken the first step by taking off your ring." He motioned towards her bare, left hand.

Surprised he'd even noticed, she shrugged. "I guess. It's just the thought of dating again is a little terrifying."

"Eventually you'll meet the right man. Who knows? He may already be in your life and you just don't know it." Before she could respond he leaned forward and lightly brushed his lips across her forehead. He turned around and pulled the comforter on the bed down.

Her skin burned where he'd kissed her. Stunned by his words and unsure of his meaning, she backed into the doorway. "Goodnight, David."

He glanced over his shoulder and shot her a quick grin, revealing one of his elusive dimples, although his dark eyes remained unreadable. "Night."

* * *

When Jade left, David stripped and got into bed. Despite the late hour and his weary body, he stared at the ceiling. The guest room didn't have a television so he didn't even have that as a distraction. He was on the right path to making sure Jade was aware of him as a man, but he worried that it wouldn't be enough. Seducing her would be tricky, but he was confident it would happen. Aware that she'd witnessed him checking her out tonight, he hadn't tried to hide his desire. He couldn't anymore. If she was ready to date, he wasn't going to stand by and watch.

He'd give her time to get used to the fact that he wanted more than just friendship. But when they crossed that line, he couldn't settle for just sex. He wanted everything and he wouldn't be someone she simply settled for.

As he stared into the darkness, a thought entered his mind. He got out of bed and rummaged in his travel bag until he found what he was looking for. He pulled out his cell and hit one of his speed dials. His friend and business partner, Nick, picked up after the second ring.

"What's up, man? I'm guessing you made it back safe?" Nick's loud voice boomed through the line.

"Yeah, I'm back at home. Listen, I'm going to be taking the next few weeks off." He hadn't had anything specific in the works that he personally needed to attend to, and he planned to spend all of his time devoted to Jade.

"Sure, no problem. You shouldn't work as much as you do anyway. We're the bosses, remember?"

"Like you listen to your own advice?"

"Yeah, yeah. I'm working on getting a team together for a trip to Panama but it's pretty standard stuff."

"Thanks man. Keep me updated with any problems." Instead of finding any solace in sleep, visions of Jade played in his mind.

Naked, erotic visions.

He wanted to stroke himself, and hated his lack of control over his body. Until the day he'd met Jade he'd been in absolute control over his dick. His palm was rough and he hated that too. He didn't want his callused hand. He wanted Jade's tight body. More than he would admit.

God, if she wasn't so damn sweet his life would have been so much easier. A pretty face he could get over. Easily. Pretty women were commonplace. She had the whole package. Looks, brains, and a heart bigger than anyone he'd met.

Long ago he'd given up feeling guilty over the thought of jerking off to her image. He couldn't help it. Her face or body entered his mind and he got hard. Instantly.

After spending time with her it was worse. His dick just went up and stayed up. Tonight was no different.

Hell, maybe tonight was worse. When she'd come home from that fucking date, he'd been floored at the sight of her. Even annoyed or angry, the woman got him positively hot. She might have been frustrated when she'd gotten home but when she'd realized he was in the hallway she'd *looked* at him.

Really, truly looked at him. He'd seen it on her face. She'd been physically aware of him. Maybe not overtly but her perception had been slightly altered. He wasn't just her friend, he was a male. Now she knew it.

As he fantasized about the color of her nipples, he had to actually bite back a groan. Would they be pink, or brown, or cherry red? He didn't care as long as she let him kiss and suck them.

Tug on them with his mouth, rake his teeth over them, until they were hard and swollen and moist from his kisses.

Sooner than later it was going to happen. Part of him knew he'd lose her friendship if he played his cards wrong and pushed her too far too fast, but something had to give. He couldn't stand by and watch her end up with someone else. Their friendship wouldn't last anyway if that happened.

Starting tomorrow, operation seduce Jade was in full effect. He was tired of using his fist and tired of being her dependable friend. One way or another he was going to find a permanent place in her bed and in her life. Or he'd just have to find a way to get over her and move on.

CHAPTER THREE

As Jade pulled out clothes from the dryer, a pair of leopard print panties fell onto the floor. She scooped the scrap of material up and for a brief moment wondered what David would think of them.

The thought was so potent, *so bizarre*, her face heated up even though she was completely alone. She absolutely did not care what he thought of her underwear.

In the midst of her cleaning she realized she hadn't heard from him since the day before. She'd taken him home, but he hadn't called all day. Not that that should surprise her. He wasn't a phone person, not even to text—which was fine with her since she didn't have that capability now anyway—and if he said he was going to pick her up for dinner, he didn't need to call and confirm. He'd be there.

Still, she missed his voice. More than she'd admit. It happened every time they got together. She was always so excited when he came back into town but when he left she got into a funk for a couple days. Now that he was actually here, she wanted to soak up all the time she could with him because she knew he'd be leaving again soon.

Yesterday all she'd been able to think about was her strange reaction to his touch, so maybe it was a good thing she hadn't heard from him.

When her house phone rang she nearly jumped out of her skin, but she smiled when her sister's name popped up on the caller ID. "Hey."

"Hey yourself. How was the date?" Maya asked.

"Long and annoying." A bad date wasn't the end of the world. It was something she should probably get used to.

"That bad huh?"

"I'm going to tell Mom he wasn't my type, but I'm never letting her set me up again."

Maya snorted. "I knew you weren't going to like him, but Mom insisted. I think she just wanted to give you a practice date so you wouldn't be nervous for the next go around."

That sounded exactly like something their mother would do. Belinda, her mom, had a way of doing things her own way, even if it made no sense to her daughters or to their father.

"Bad date aside, I want to ask you something, but I don't want you jumping to any conclusions."

"All right. What's up?"

"The other night, David stayed over—"

"Whoa. *Nice.*"

Jade sighed. "Let me *finish*. He stayed in the *guest* room Friday night because after we were through catching up, it was too late to drive him home. I know it sounds crazy, but I think I saw him checking me out."

"How exactly?" Maya asked cautiously.

"I caught him blatantly staring at my butt. Not leering or anything, but he was definitely staring. Intently. Like he wanted to, you know…"

Maya chuckled lightly. "Well, you do have a nice ass. It runs in the family."

Jade rolled her eyes, even though she wasn't going to deny it. The Bancroft women were all slim and small breasted. However, their backsides were a different story. No amount of exercise reduced the size of their hips or butts. "That's not the point."

"I know it's not. What do you want me to say? Do you want me to assure you that you're mistaken, because, sweetie, I have a feeling that he was most definitely checking you out. David wants you in a bad way, and I'm surprised it's taken you this long to figure it out. No, I take that back. I'm surprised it's taken *him* this long to do anything about it."

A rush of heat swept over her. She wasn't sure she liked where this conversation was heading. "What are you talking about?"

"Look, I'm not saying I know anything for sure. I don't get to see the two of you together very often, but I do know that man thinks the world of you and would probably give up his left nut to sleep with you."

Jade choked on her sweet tea.

"Hey, you wanted honesty, and that's what I'm giving you. David is interested in you, and in my opinion, he has been for quite some time. You're just too blind to see it."

"What is it with men and their left nut anyway? Why not the right one? Or both of them?" she muttered. Talking about this was better than talking about David.

"I don't know. I've asked Colin about that, and he has no sufficient answer. Don't get off the subject. What are you going to do about this?"

Do? Was her sister crazy? "I'm not going to do *anything* about this. There are at least three very strong reasons I can think of why we would never work, and I'm not willing to throw away our friendship over sex. I know my hormones have been a little wacky lately, but I'm not that desperate."

David was Aidan's best friend, he wasn't the type of man to settle down, and, oh yeah, he was *Aidan's best friend*. It could never work with them, and for all she knew, he was just being a typical man and admiring what had been placed in front of him. Did she think he was attractive? Sure. She'd have to be blind not to, but they were friends.

"Who says it would end with sex, Jade? I don't think he's looking for a one night stand."

"Well, I seriously doubt he's looking to settle down. He's almost forty, and I've never known him to stay in a relationship longer than a few weeks. And I'm being generous with that length of time. Not that that even *matters*. This conversation is so stupid it's not even funny." Talking about sex and David in the same sentence was making her whole body flush.

"All I'm saying is, don't ignore his presence in your life. He could be exactly what you're looking for… Listen, I need to get off the phone. It's been quiet around here for too long. I've got to check on the boys.""

Once they'd disconnected Jade glared at the silent portable. "Well, you were no help."

"Maya giving you trouble again?" A deep voice from behind caused her to scream and jump out of her chair. She moved with such speed, the chair toppled on its side, and she nearly lost her footing.

"Are you trying to give me a heart attack?" She clutched the phone to her chest and pushed David square in the middle of his chest as she tried to steady her breathing. She knew her face had to be bright red.

"I knocked a few times and tried the doorbell." He shrugged but didn't look the least bit apologetic. "The front door was open, so I let myself in. You need to start locking your doors." He took a sip from a fresh glass of ice tea, which let Jade know that he'd been there for at least a few minutes. How much had he heard exactly?

"I didn't hear you knock." She wrapped her arms around her chest. She wasn't wearing a bra underneath her t-shirt. Normally she wouldn't have cared, but with Maya's words fresh on her brain, she was very aware of her state of dress. David standing in front of her wearing a navy blue crewneck fleece stretched across his muscled torso, looking good enough to eat, didn't help either.

His lips twitched, as if he was fighting a smile. "Obviously. I couldn't get you on the phone, and I wanted to give you this before tonight." He held out a sleek looking cell phone with a wide face. It had a hard cover with black and pink skull and crossbones on it.

"Skulls?" She couldn't hide the amusement in her voice. When she reached out to take it a breeze blew up, and she felt her nipples harden. She forced herself not to think about it but they got even harder.

He held up his hands in mock surrender. "I didn't know what to get you, and the woman at the store assured me you would love the case. But if not, there are a lot more to choose from."

"No, this is perfect. Thanks, I really do appreciate it. Do I need to call and set up a number or something?" She used her computer to keep inventory at work, ran her own website and she was more than proficient at paying all her bills on-line. However, she'd had her old phone for so long this thing was like alien technology. Considering it had taken her an embarrassing amount of time to figure out how to download songs to her iPod, she figured there would be a learning curve to this.

"No, I've already taken care of that, and I paid for the first month. All the information is in here." He held up a small shopping bag. "You can transfer everything to your name this week."

"You didn't have to do that. I'll pay you back whatever it cost."

His lips pulled into a thin line. "No. I did this for my peace of mind. I can't stand the thought of you walking home every night without a phone."

He had the same expression of fierce determination on his face that he had about a year and a half ago when he'd dragged her out of bed, thrown her into the shower fully clothed, and told her to stop feeling sorry for herself. That had been such a dark time in her life and he'd been the exact kind of friend she'd needed then. If giving her this was *that* important to him, why waste her breath? Especially when the gesture was so sweet.

"Okay. Thank you then."

"I just wanted to stop by and give you that. I've got a few errands to run before dinner. What time did you want me to pick you up?"

She glanced at her watch as she followed him to the kitchen. It was three o'clock, and she still needed to finish cleaning and go over her books at the store. "How about seven?"

"Works for me." He drained his glass and placed it in the sink. She walked him to the front door but he paused in the entryway. There was something intense in his dark eyes. She couldn't figure out what he was thinking but the heated look he gave her made her knees weaken. "Lock the door after me. Anyone could have walked into your house today, Jade. I know you live in a safe area, but anything can happen."

"I know, I will." When he'd gone, she slipped the lock into place.

* * *

David kicked his truck into gear and headed to the supermarket. As he pulled away from Jade's house, he couldn't stop frowning. Something intangible wormed its way into his brain.

She'd acted on edge around him, and he couldn't figure out why. She hadn't done anything specific, but he'd noticed the defensive way she'd crossed her arms over her chest, as if protecting herself. But from what, *him*? The thought was ludicrous.

And it wasn't like her. Normally she greeted him with a giant hug or a kiss on the cheek, and she hadn't done either today. Body language was something he'd learned to read well over the years. Jade had never put up any walls against him, and it worried him that she was now. Especially when he planned to tell her how he felt.

His cell phone rang just as he finished loading the last of the groceries into the back of his truck. He glanced down before answering and his entire body heated when he saw Jade's number. He knew he had serious problems if that's all it took to get him worked up. "Hey."

"How'd you know it was me?" Jade asked.

"I programmed your new number into my phone when I bought yours. Everything okay?"

"I was just talking to Maya, and I didn't realize it was Super Bowl Sunday. Do you want to skip going out and watch the game at your house?"

David knew how she felt about football or any sport for that matter. Her voluntary offer to watch it surprised him. "Are you sure? I know it's not your favorite sport."

She laughed. "Yes, I'm sure. Besides, I like the commercials. Don't worry about picking me up though. It doesn't make sense for you to drive over here then back to your place."

"All right, I'll see you in a few hours." After he disconnected he couldn't get over the sensation that tonight was it. Tonight he was going to make his move.

* * *

Jade shut her refrigerator door then sighed. She still had a million things to do before tonight.

Startled at a sound, she turned to find David standing in the doorway.

He somehow looked larger than life. And he wasn't wearing a shirt. What the hell? Was she dreaming?

"What are you doing here?" she asked.

He didn't answer.

Frowning, she walked across the kitchen toward him and she felt like she was walking on a cloud. David hadn't said a word. Just stared at her with those dark eyes. Dark eyes filled with dark, delicious promises. Her stomach muscles tightened. Where had that thought come from?

Before she could move, he came at her. Fast. Not giving her a chance to move, he covered her mouth with hard, demanding lips.

Somehow, his kiss was still gentle. Which seemed impossible. And crazy. David was kissing her.

David.

His tongue swept over hers in erotic, sensual swipes. Despite his tenderness, he invaded her mouth and her senses with no mercy.

Her abdomen clenched as his hands found their way to her hips. He grasped her as his tongue danced against hers. When he pulled away she thought he was going to stop but he just continued kissing along her jaw. She shivered as a traitorous heat bloomed between her thighs.

"Do you know how long I've wanted to do this," he murmured close to her ear. "I want you naked and under me so bad it hurts."

His words and his kisses seemed to envelope her. Like a warm cocoon they wrapped around her, making her lightheaded.

She knew she should push him away but couldn't force herself to move. She loved the way he ran his tongue and teeth over her neck. Arching into him, she rubbed her aching breasts against his chest, letting him know how much she enjoyed it. Until he'd touched her she hadn't realized how much she'd wanted this.

Needed this.

He murmured something else against the pulse point in her neck but she couldn't understand him. The blood rushed in her ears too loudly. She didn't care what he'd said anyway. All she cared about was the unbearable heat building between her legs. She'd forgotten what this hot sensation felt like. Forgot what it was like to have a man get her off.

When his hands tightened around her hips she tensed. In one quick swoop he lifted her up so that she was sitting on the edge of the granite island.

"David—"

"Let me do this for you. Please." He sounded as if he'd swallowed gravel.

His entire body stilled as he stared at her, waiting for an answer. This was her dead husband's best friend. What the hell was she doing?

David's hands were firmly wrapped around her hips but she knew if she said to stop he would. It was the please that ultimately made her say yes. That and the heat burning in his eyes. She'd never imagined to see something so potent from him but she found it got her hotter than she wanted to admit.

"Okay," she whispered. Everything about the moment was so intimate. She wasn't quite sure what he wanted to do but something deep inside her told her she'd like whatever it was.

Without taking his eyes off her, he pulled her flimsy shorts down her legs and tossed them to the side. When he traced his finger along the thin strap of her bikini cut panties she shivered. It had been so long since she'd let a man touch her yet this felt like coming home. In a strange, totally messed up way, this felt right.

She knew it was stupid to let David do this. They were friends. Best friends.

But he felt so good.

His callused finger pushed the material aside and he tweaked her clit. Just a gentle, teasing rub. The pressure was perfect. She wanted more of it.

When she moistened her lips his dark eyes narrowed on them but he didn't stop what he was doing. David slightly increased the pressure on her clit, rubbing back and forth in a torturous rhythm.

It was enough to get her hot but not quite enough to push her over the edge. Her inner muscles contracted, begging for that climax.

He leaned forward a few inches and lightly covered her mouth with his. When he tugged her bottom lip between his teeth she shuddered.

"Lay back," he murmured against her mouth.

Jade froze at his words.

As if he understood her wariness, his finger dipped lower, away from her clit until he pushed inside her.

The intrusion was more than welcome. Needed even. She was already soaking wet. Her inner muscles clamped around him.

She felt so exposed under the bright lights of the kitchen but she laid back against the counter. The island top chilled her back. It was in direct contrast to the heat surging through her veins. Her nipples hardened painfully against the soft material of her top.

His breath was hot against her spread legs and inner thighs. When he moaned against one of her legs, she felt it straight to her core.

He still had one finger buried inside her as he began trailing kisses across her mound. Though he avoided her clit, she knew he was just teasing her.

"Just as perfect as I thought you'd be," he murmured against her bare skin.

Savoring his kisses and attention, she scooted a few inches lower, desperate to ease the throbbing ache.

When he withdrew his finger, her vagina clenched but his tongue delved between her folds, stroking in and out. She arched her back and nearly vaulted off the countertop when he lightly squeezed her clit between this thumb and forefinger.

With his tongue, he continued his insistent assault. The strokes were both torturous and scorching. And with his finger, he tweaked and rubbed the raw bundle of nerves until she was panting. He moved against the nub in a measured, circular motion that was perfect.

"More." She didn't care if she begged. She wanted her release. After years of being alone, years of feeling nothing but grief and sadness, she needed this. She wanted to lose herself in the pleasure David was giving her.

Shifting up, he sucked on her already hardened clit and penetrated her with two fingers. The abrupt action was welcome.

She grasped at the unforgiving surface beneath her. Needing to hold something, she clutched onto David's head as her inner walls convulsed out of control.

Her hips pumped against his fingers and mouth until she couldn't hold herself back any longer. Crying out, she let go and fell over the edge. As she surged into climax, a kaleidoscope of colors flashed in front of her for a brief moment. With a small cry, her abdomen clenched one last time before she fell boneless against the hard counter.

Jade's eyes flew open. "Holy hell," she muttered to the empty living room. Talk about intense.

She was breathing hard and her nipples painfully rubbed against her shirt with each intake. It was a tired cliché but they were so hard they probably could cut glass.

Embarrassed, she withdrew her hand from her shorts. She shivered as her finger rubbed over her swollen clit. Her panties were damp and soaked with her juices. She couldn't remember the last time she'd ever had a dream so vivid, so intense. Certainly not one in which she'd actually masturbated. *And climaxed.*

And never one that starred David.

Her inner walls clenched as she thought about what she'd imagined him doing to her. Looking around her living room she realized she must have dozed off while folding laundry. Piles of towels sat next to her on the couch.

Her house was quiet. As it should be.

What the hell was wrong with her? She really must need sex more than she'd realized if she was imagining David going down on her.

Even though she was alone, her cheeks flushed as she thought about seeing him in a few hours. Thank God the man wasn't a mind reader.

CHAPTER FOUR

Jade arrived right before kickoff with a bag of Chinese food. How the hell was she ever going to look at him straight after that intense dream? After giving David a brief hug, she handed him the two takeout bags and tried to ignore the rare, completely feminine reaction in her stomach. "I know you didn't ask, but I figured you didn't have much in the way of food here."

"I didn't until today. Now I'm stocked for at least a month." When she raised her eyebrows, he answered her unspoken question. "I'm taking an extended vacation."

"Oh." The word stuck in her throat. She'd expected him to leave in a day or two. Like usual. Then everything would go back to normal and these weird feelings she had would go back into hibernation.

She shifted her feet as the image of his appreciative look from the night before, and her sister's words, flashed through her mind. She needed to get over whatever *this* was. This was *David*, and she didn't like the tingling sensation in the pit of her stomach every time she saw him. It was just as unsettling that she now noticed how very male he was. She'd always known he was attractive, but knowing and being aware of him as a sexual being were two very different things.

One of his dark eyebrows arched. "You sound almost disappointed that I'll be around."

Averting her gaze, she brushed past him and headed towards the kitchen. She tried to ignore the spicy masculine scent that seemed to permeate everything. "You know that's not what I meant. I'm just surprised, that's all. You're normally only in town for a few days at a time."

"I've decided to make some changes. The first one being that I won't be traveling as much. I guess we'll be seeing a lot more of each other." Something about the tone of his voice was almost sensual, inviting. Maybe even challenging.

No. that had to be her imagination. After that stupid, erotic dream she wanted to scream. David did *not* want her. Not like that.

His spacious kitchen was large enough to hold at least ten people comfortably. Except today. Today the walls were closing in. She moved over to the breakfast nook in an effort to put some distance between them. "Uh, that's great, David."

An erratic rhythm pounded against her rib cage, and even though it was ridiculous, she was fearful he could somehow hear it. She cleared her throat. "Do you mind if I grab a bottle of water from the fridge?"

"Help yourself. I didn't know you were bringing anything, and I've already got some burgers out on the grill. Which do you want?"

"Burgers sound great. I'll just put this up. You can have it for lunch tomorrow." She busied herself putting up the food until she heard the sound of the sliding glass door open and close. Then she shut the door to the stainless steel fridge and allowed herself to breathe. Instead of following him outside, she walked over to the entryway. Since his back was facing her, she peered at him through the glass unseen. She'd always been aware that he was good looking, but it was hard to believe she'd never noticed how utterly masculine he was until recently.

Broad, muscular shoulders strained against his plain green polo T-shirt, and his jeans hung perfectly on equally muscular legs. He had what her sister called a baseball player's butt. Nice, firm, and perfectly rounded. She could just imagine how nice it would be to...Stop, stop, stop! She mentally berated herself and shook those thoughts free before she started undressing him with her eyes. *Again.*

This wasn't a road she dared travel down. She couldn't act on it. David was a friend, a good friend on whom she'd come to depend immensely. She wasn't about to do something to screw that up because her hormones were a little loopy.

Thirty minutes later, David sat on his brown leather sofa, and she stretched her legs out the length of the matching love seat. David watched the game and she tried to read a magazine but kept dozing off. She was full from the food and even though she loved his company, football could put her in a coma.

"I'll never understand your fascination with this game." She muttered mainly to herself, but loud enough for him to hear.

"Well, I'll never understand your obsession with shoes. No one should have ten pairs of black heels." His lips curved up into a grin.

"That shows how little you understand women, my friend." A loud yawn escaped before she could stop herself.

His eyebrows drew together. "Have you not been sleeping well, or is the game really that boring?"

She'd certainly gotten a nap this afternoon. Of course it hadn't done anything but get her worked up. "My sleep has been fine. I just haven't been getting a lot of it. I've been working on new designs practically every night after work and before I know it, it's after midnight... But yes, the game is *that* boring."

All she received was a snort.

Jade loved her job and turned a nice profit, but for a while she'd been contemplating creating her own line of clothing and accessories inspired by the Florida lifestyle. "I don't even know how I'm going to find time to date. I should probably hire someone else at the store."

"Has your mom or sister set you up with anyone else?" he asked with hardly any inflection.

Her sister *must* be wrong. If he was asking her about dating life, he obviously wasn't interested himself. Even if he had been checking her out, that didn't mean anything. He might be one of her best friends, but he was still a man. What did she expect? And why was she disappointed that he didn't care? She seriously needed her head examined. "No, and I don't think I'm going to trust my mom anymore. Not after that last disaster."

"What about Maya?" He picked up her empty water bottle, his empty beer bottle, and a half-eaten bowl of popcorn.

"She only knows cops."

"What does that have to do with anything?" He leaned against the edge of the couch.

"I told her I don't want anyone with a dangerous job."

"What exactly do you want?"

She shrugged, feeling a little self-conscious. "For starters, he needs a job."

"But not a dangerous one?" A smile tugged at the corners of his mouth.

"That's right. Nothing that keeps me up at night. I loved Aidan, but I'm over that constant worrying."

"What else?" His words almost sounded like a growl.

She cleared her throat. "It's not like I have a laminated list or anything. I just want a decent man who opens doors for me, who shares the same morals, who I actually like and I want him to treat me like an equal. He needs to be faithful...and the sex needs to be amazing."

His eyes widened slightly. "Is that all?"

"Hey, you asked. I'm tired of living like a nun. Oh yeah, and he needs to appreciate my shoe obsession." When he rolled his eyes, she tossed a throw pillow at him before returning to her magazine.

David expertly ducked out of the way and walked to the kitchen laughing under his breath. As he threw their trash away he fought the hard-on straining against his jeans. When Jade said she wanted hot sex it had taken every ounce of will power he had not to show any visible reaction. Well, other than the one in his pants. The thought of her dating was bad enough, but the thought of her sleeping...no, he couldn't let his mind wander down that dark road.

Fifteen years ago, he'd endured twenty five weeks of intensive training in the form of BUD/S to become a Navy SEAL. He could kill a man with his bare hands at least twenty different ways, he could survive—and had—for months behind enemy lines on any terrain with little to no food or water and could navigate for miles in the ocean in absolute darkness. Now he ran a successful security organization with jobs all over the globe, yet somehow, he couldn't ask Jade on a date. A simple question. Would you like to go to dinner? Maybe see a movie afterwards? He was pathetic.

He returned with a new beer, but his hard-on wouldn't go away. If anything, he felt like it was getting bigger. "Isn't that the singer you like so much?" The halftime show was on, and a petite blonde singer was running around in bare feet from one end of the stage to the other. "Jade?"

The only response he received was her steady breathing. He peered over the love seat to find her curled up with a magazine in her lap, eyes closed. Without disturbing her, he removed the magazine from her hands and pulled an afghan down over her. He lifted her feet and sank down on the end of the couch. Her feet twitched in his lap and he resisted the urge to touch them. God, even her *feet* turned him on. Soft, delicate, just like her. He tried to concentrate on the game, but his eyes kept drifting back to her still figure.

He'd always had fantasies about her but lately they'd been worse. Technicolor worse. His dreams were vivid and 3-D, including tastes, sounds, and scent. Right down to the coconut shampoo she used. The sounds were probably the worst because in real time when he saw her he could picture her moaning underneath him, on top of him, on his couch, his bed, wherever.

Everywhere.

Anywhere.

The game finally ended so he flipped off the television and gently touched her arm. Jade." On the short loveseat he didn't have to stretch far. Instead of opening her eyes, she just pulled the blanket tighter around her shoulders and mumbled something unintelligible. "Jade, the game's over."

This time he shook her a little harder. When she didn't move, he fingered a loose tendril of hair and lightly caressed her cheek, letting his hand trace down her delicate jaw. Her skin was satiny against his callused fingers. He'd pay for it later, late at night when she consumed his thoughts, but he wanted to feel her. To experience the torture of touching her skin.

"The game's over, Jade."

Her green eyes fluttered open, and she stared at him in slight confusion. She ran a hand through her rumpled hair and partially sat up. She stretched her legs out across his lap. "Is the game already over?"

He nodded because he didn't trust his voice. As if they had a mind of their own, his hands grabbed one of her feet. The most primal part of him savored holding onto her like this. She was his and it felt right to touch her this way.

Her lips slightly parted as he started to massage her foot. "Wow."

"Feel good?" he murmured.

Jade's green eyes flared as she mutely nodded.

Using the base of his palm, he increased pressure as he kneaded the underside of her foot. As he worked her pressure points, her pink tongue darted out and drew a slow line along her bottom lip.

His shifted against his seat as he watched her. He wanted to feel that tongue trace down his hard length. When her breathing became more shallow he knew she was getting turned on. Hell, she might not even realize it but he could see the subtle changes in her body language.

She squirmed against the couch as she stared at his hands on her foot. As if she were mesmerized.

David wanted to say something. Anything. Nothing he came up with sounded particularly suave. And he didn't want to break the moment. He couldn't believe she hadn't pulled away yet. Besides, he was better with his hands. He decided to let them do the talking.

Taking a chance, he moved higher until he held on to one of her calves. She tensed for a moment but didn't pull back or tell him to stop. When he started to rub the firm muscles of her lower leg she leaned back and pushed out a slow, unsteady breath. His touch wasn't necessarily intimate but every single one of his muscles tightened as he ran his hands over her smooth skin.

Jade wasn't sure what David was doing but she couldn't tell him to stop. It was as if she'd gone mute. That dream had really rattled her, but this was definitely no dream. This was real. Very, very real.

Inside she felt as tense as a spring but what he was doing with his hands was amazing, soothing. The way he handled her was so gentle and caring she couldn't tear her gaze away from his hands on her body.

He pushed the afghan blanket up as he worked on her calves, slowly revealing more of her skin. In that instant she was thankful she'd shaved.

A rush of warmth flooded between her thighs as he moved to the next leg and continued the same torturous assault. He was the first man to touch her in two years and everything about what he was doing felt right.

So right it scared her.

Some part of her thought she should tell him to stop. Pull her feet away and simply sit upright. But she couldn't. She ached for him to keep going higher and higher.

She could just imagine one of his skilled hands covering her mound. Teasing her lips open. Rubbing her clit and pushing deep inside her. It had been too long since she'd felt that sort of connection with anyone. The thought made her want to moan out loud. If he did, she wondered if it would feel better than what she'd imagined.

She dug her fingers into the loveseat when his fingers inched higher. Why couldn't she tear her eyes away? Her nipples strained against her bra but she was thankful she wore one. She slightly shifted and the peaked buds rubbed against her bra cups. The action was mildly arousing. It would feel a whole lot better if it was David's tongue flicking over her nipples. The thought sent a burst of heat surging through her.

Now he was most definitely edging into dangerous territory. There was nothing friendly about the way his callused hands moved up until he was rubbing her inner thigh. He was closer to her knee than the junction between her thighs but he'd crossed that invisible line. Friends did not touch each other this way. Not above the knee.

It was too intimate. Too...something. Her eyes were heavy lidded as she watched him push the blanket up even farther. He could probably see her panties by now. Instead of embarrassment, she felt empowered. Wondered if he liked what he saw.

She also wondered what they were doing. Dreams didn't have consequences. If they took this further, things would change between them.

When his fingers trailed a few inches higher, her gaze snapped up to meet his. She found him watching her intently, questioningly. His dark eyes were heated and full of lust. It made her brain short circuit. What was she supposed to say when the feel of his fingers inching higher and higher made her wonder if she might dissolve into a puddle of mush if he *didn't* keep going.

He lifted one of her legs and moved so that he was now sitting in between them. It didn't even cross her mind to tell him to stop. His fingers were no longer massaging her.

Now they were boldly trailing up her inner thigh with determination. His dark eyes stayed on hers the whole time. She wanted to look somewhere else but couldn't. In a weird way she felt as if she were looking at a stranger.

A really hot stranger she trusted with her life. This was a new side to him. One she found she wanted to get to know.

When one of his fingers played with the edge of her panties she jerked. But he didn't stop. He cupped her mound and rubbed his palm against it. The pressure was so perfect she gasped. He wasn't even touching her clit but the grinding motion of his palm was almost enough to make her lose control.

With his free hand he pushed the afghan blanket completely off her and onto the floor. Before she hadn't been able to see what he was doing but now she was exposed.

Vulnerable.

Her throat clenched as she stared at the display they made. Her legs were spread and her dress was pushed to her upper thighs. Almost exactly like she'd fantasized. David's strong hand disappeared underneath the edge of her dress.

"What..." She didn't know what she wanted to ask. Maybe what he planned to do. The words wouldn't form on her lips though. She didn't want to ask because she didn't want him to stop. And she was afraid if she said too much, she'd start thinking too much and realize how crazy this was.

Suddenly he moved so that he was kneeling on the floor next to the couch and he withdrew his hand. The loss of his touch made her feel cold.

He patted the ground next to him. "I want you stretched out here."

His deep voice sent a tremble rolling through her. He'd never talked to her like that before but the command in his tone guaranteed she'd do practically anything he asked. Or ordered as it were.

As she moved, the leather against her bare skin felt cool but did little to douse her raging insides. It was as if the blood in her veins was scorching and she'd burst into flames at any moment if he didn't... She didn't know *what* she wanted him to do. She just needed that ache burning deep inside her to be eased.

When she moved to the floor as he ordered, she laid back. Before she could think about what they were doing, he slipped his hands under her dress again and grasped the edge of her panties. He quickly tugged them down and tossed them somewhere. She didn't really care where.

She tried to sit up, but he shook his head. "Lay back and just enjoy what I'm doing."

There he went again with that commanding voice. She liked this side of him.

Two strong hands settled on the inside of her thighs and she trembled. She couldn't help it. The shudder just rolled through her all the way to her toes. The not seeing, the not knowing what was coming next was a strange aphrodisiac. It was weird, they hadn't even kissed yet but she was letting him touch her most intimate area.

David stared at the folds between Jade's legs and fought to breathe. Somewhere in the back of his head he wondered if this was even real. If he was possibly having one of those damn dreams again.

With his finger he traced his finger down her slit.

She jerked at the sudden touch and let out a tiny panting sound. And she was wet. Very, very wet. Yep, this was real.

Breathing in her sweet scent, he leaned forward and tasted what he'd been dreaming about for longer than he wanted to admit. He ran his tongue up her slit and she rolled her hips against his mouth.

The action made him smile. He'd worried that he might be taking things too far but it was obvious she was into this. Into him.

This was going so much better than he'd hoped.

As he traced his tongue around her pulsing clit she let out this erotic sound he couldn't describe. It was something between a sigh and a moan. "David." She said his name loud and clear.

Hearing *his* name on her lips did something to him. It was so primal it scared the shit out of him. He wanted to claim her. Mark her somehow. Make it so that any man knew she was his. And instead of his tongue, he wanted to sink his cock into her. Wanted to feel her tight sheath clench around him as she raked her fingers down his back.

For now, this would do. He was going to play this right. He had to if he wanted a repeat performance.

Using his tongue, he increased the pressure on her clit. Over and over he circled and teased the hard bud. With each flick she trembled even more.

"Just like that." Her voice was hoarse, unsteady.

She was so close. With every tremble and jerk she made he could tell it wouldn't take much to push her into climax. Part of him wanted to stretch this out as long as possible but she was like a live wire and he desperately needed to see her come.

He inserted his finger and couldn't stop the groan that erupted when she clamped around him. One wasn't enough. He slid another one in and she vaulted upward. With his free hand he laid a soothing hand on her abdomen and pressed down. He didn't want her trying to hold onto her control. She was like that. Wanted everything in her life nice and tidy.

Nothing about what they were doing would fit into her orderly world but that was all changing. Slowly, he started to move his fingers in and out of her. It was gradual but he could feel the tension leaving her body.

Feel her letting go of all that control.

Her inner walls clamped around his fingers and her back arched so he continued teasing her clit. Tighter and tighter she clenched until finally she grasped onto his head. Her fingers threaded through his hair and she squeezed lightly.

With a muted shout her hips lifted off the ground as her juices covered his fingers and her climax rolled through her.

"No more. Too much," she gasped out as she fell back against the carpet.

Though he didn't want to, he pulled his fingers out of her as she came down from her high. As she panted, he placed soft kisses along her inner thighs and down her legs. The scent of sex and her desire surrounded them. It was almost enough to make him come then and there.

This had definitely changed everything between them. He'd known it was coming but hadn't expected it tonight. Definitely hadn't expected this. Damn, he hadn't even kissed her properly yet.

That was about to change now.

Sitting up, he moved so that he was on top of her. Using his elbows he kept himself propped up. His covered erection moved against her mound and her legs widened around him. If only he didn't have jeans on. He could slide right into her. She'd been tight around his fingers so he knew she'd clamp around his cock like a vise.

Panic glittered in her wide eyes as she stared at him. He'd seen that look before on the battlefield. It was fear. Raw and real. Something he'd never wanted or imagined to see from her. It happened so suddenly he hadn't expected it.

"Jade. I—"

"Oh my God," she breathed out. "Oh. My. *God.*" Moving lightning fast, she shimmied out from under him and scrambled to her feet. She tugged on her dress and looked down at herself in horror.

He followed suit and tried to track her movements as she hurried around his living room. "Jade, what are you doing?"

She wouldn't meet his gaze as she scooped her purse up from underneath the coffee table. "That was so not a dream. That was real. Real, real, real. I can't believe we just did that."

"Well we did," he ground out.

She muttered something under her breath as she shoved her panties into her purse.

"Jade? I have your shoes." His words forced her to turn around. He held out flat sandals, which she took without saying anything.

"Thanks," she mumbled, but *still* wouldn't meet his gaze. She fumbled around in her purse for her keys.

He reached out and closed his hand around hers once she pulled them out. She wasn't leaving like this. "Are you so surprised this happened?"

The past couple days, hell, months, had been building up to this moment. She might not be prepared for the truth, but they were right together. He was sick of carrying this burden and sick of denying his feelings for her.

"This was a mistake." Long, heavy lashes lifted and their gazes collided. The words came out as a whisper and almost seemed to stick in her throat.

"Mistake?" he growled.

She took an involuntary step back. The small action was a clear message to him. He moved back to give her room. He knew her better than anyone. All his instincts told him to crowd her, make her talk, but she looked like a scared animal. The fear in her eyes *almost* pissed him off though.

He wasn't sure what the hell she was so afraid of. "You liked what I did."

Her face flamed bright crimson. Her brow crinkled together, and she opened her mouth to speak, but all she managed was, "I'm sorry."

He watched her turn and leave. She paused once in the entryway to the front door but didn't turn around. Whatever she'd been contemplating, she changed her mind.

David started to go after her but stopped mid step. He'd been hiding his feelings for years. Even if she'd had some sort of awareness of him the past couple days, the feelings were definitely new to her. And he knew she hadn't let a man touch her in two years so while every primal instinct inside him told him to chase after her and kiss her until neither of them could think, he resisted. She needed to clear her head. He'd give her some time—a day at most—but then he was staking his claim.

Things weren't over between them. Not by a long shot.

CHAPTER FIVE

Jade took a steadying breath and bent to retie her running shoes. She cranked up the volume to her iPod and continued jogging. The blaring music drowned out the typical early morning sounds. Unfortunately, it couldn't silence her thoughts. Nothing could do that.

She was the worst kind of coward. Last night David given her the most intense orgasm she'd had in a while and when he'd moved on top of her she'd known without a doubt he was going to kiss her. He'd been looming over her all she'd been able to think was 'this was David'. *David.* She'd let him kiss her most intimate area then when he'd simply wanted to kiss her lips she'd freaked.

A rush of guilt had bowled her over as she thought about kissing her dead husband's best friend. She knew Aidan was gone and wasn't coming back but something in her head had screamed 'red alert' and she'd shut down. Now she just wanted to cry over the hurt she'd seen in David's eyes. Instead of explaining things she'd run out.

David deserved better than what she'd done. *So much better.*

The sun peeked out from behind one of the dangerously dark clouds, and a glance at her watch reminded her she needed to get back home soon if she wanted to get to work on time. More importantly, she wanted to stop by David's first. She owed him that courtesy. And a heck of a lot more. If she didn't see him immediately, she wouldn't be able to think of anything else all day. It didn't matter that she had no clue what to say. All that mattered was seeing him. And apologizing.

Profusely.

An hour later, she steered into David's gravelly driveway and reminded herself to breathe for the hundredth time in the past ten minutes. She stopped the engine and held onto her keys so tightly she was afraid she'd draw blood.

Though sorely tempted to turn around, she ordered her legs to move. The walk down the stone steps to his front door was a short one. Too short. Her stomach roiled, but she managed to lift her leaden arm to knock. After what felt like an eternity, the door flew open.

"Can I help you?" A tall, lithe, blonde woman stood in front of her wearing a haughty expression and not much else. Every inch of skin not already bare was visible through the black matching bra and panty set. The sheer material wrapped around the woman's supermodel form like a second skin, showcasing perfect breasts and curves.

Jade had to blink to make sure she wasn't seeing things. The woman was real all right. Bile and an unexpected surge of potent jealousy rose in Jade's throat. It hurt to speak but she found her voice. To her horror, her words came out hoarse and scratchy. "I came to see David."

"He's in the shower, but I can get him for you if you don't mind waiting." The woman lifted a perfect, waxed eyebrow, leaned against the door frame with her perfectly toned body, and crossed her perfect arms over her perfect chest.

Jade wanted to throw up. She willed the ground to swallow her whole. When that didn't happen, she managed to squeeze out a few more words. "No, don't worry about it. I...I'll just catch him later."

The woman didn't answer. She stood there for a moment with one eyebrow raised in amusement on her heart-shaped face. Then she pivoted on her heel and slammed the door in Jade's face. Without hesitation, Jade turned and fled back down the palm-tree-lined walkway to her car. Rocks spewed everywhere as she tore out of his driveway. She tried to rein in the tears, but they were streaming down her face by the time she hit the Usina Bridge.

She certainly had no claim on David. He was free to sleep with whoever he wanted. Still, a cold knot formed in her stomach. The farther she drove, the tighter it stretched and the more painful it became. Last night he'd looked at her like she was the most precious possession in the world, and even though she hadn't admitted it then, even to herself, she liked it. Maybe even craved it. She was *so* stupid. How could she have been so wrong about him? The desire she'd seen in his eyes last night had been real, like scary real. He'd wanted her in a bad way. Of that she was certain. And if she hadn't been, the erection she'd felt when he'd moved on top of her was proof enough. A man couldn't fake something like that.

When she pulled into her driveway she was even more confused than when she left. It would be so easy to drown in her thoughts if she allowed it. A brisk walk would clear her mind. She grabbed her purse and started the walk to work while trying not to think about David and what a bastard he was.

Unfortunately that was all she did.

When her cell phone rang, an irrational hope sprang up that it was David. Immediately she wanted to kick herself. The guy was a liar. A big one. She didn't want to hear his stupid voice. Despite her dark mood she smiled when she checked the caller id.

"Hey, Maya."

"Hey, you want to have lunch today? I just spoke to Mom and she's free too."

"Sure. Oh, by the way, remember that man you wanted to set me up with, Rick something? If he's still available, I'm ready."

"It's Rick Mancino, and he's definitely still available. He's been pestering me non-stop to set him up ever since he saw your picture. Why the sudden change of heart? What happened to your no cop rule?"

Jade didn't feel like telling her sister what she'd just seen or what she'd done the night before, but Maya would drag it out of her eventually. For the sake of time and sanity she decided to give up the battle before it started. "To keep this very short, last night David and I uh, fooled around a little but I freaked out and left." Her sister gasped, but Jade didn't give her a chance to interrupt. She'd reacted poorly and didn't want to relive it.

"Wait, it gets better. This morning when I stopped by to talk to him about it, a half-naked woman answered the door looking very satisfied."

"What?" Maya gasped.

"You heard right. I'm such an idiot, and I hate that I even care." She cared so much more than she could have imagined. A lump the size of a baseball had settled in her throat, and it was taking all the energy she possessed not to break down in tears. The thought of him with another woman tore at her heart and brought up feelings of inadequacy and jealousy she didn't know she had. He hadn't brought another woman around in…she racked her brain to remember a time. Dang, had it really been two years? It was selfish, she knew, but she'd always thought of him as belonging to her. Not in the boyfriend sense, but he was always around. Always there when she needed him. Looking at her car when she had trouble, or checking out her air conditioning when she asked.

"What did this skank look like?"

Jade snorted, which earned her a strange look from an elderly couple out for a morning stroll. "She was fucking gorgeous. I'm talking Victoria's Secret model gorgeous."

Maya laughed which only spurred Jade's annoyance. "Why is that funny?"

"Oh, I'm not laughing at your story. I just don't think I've heard you say fuck since you were sixteen. It didn't sound right then, and it sounds even more ridiculous now."

"Damn it, Maya, don't try to make me feel better or change the subject. I know exactly what you're doing."

"Wow, you cursed twice in one conversation. I think that's a new record for you."

Despite her heavy heart, her mood slightly improved. But not by much. "You're impossible. I just got to the store, but come by around eleven and we'll take an early lunch. Hopefully we'll beat the crowd."

"See you then. And if you're sure about the whole date thing, I'll talk to Colin and see when Rick is available."

"I *so* am." Jade fumbled around in her oversized purse for her keys and finally located them. Once inside, she scowled at her bright, airy store. The front windows faced east so she didn't bother turning any lights on this early in the morning. The light cast against the pale yellow walls created an airy atmosphere that normally relaxed her.

Today, she didn't want to see anyone.

Pam strolled in a little after eleven o'clock, just as Jade put the finishing touches on a new accessory display case. Her young employee looked beautiful as always, but the dark circles under her eyes were a giveaway that she desperately needed a huge cup of coffee. And maybe a shot of espresso.

"Hey, Pam, long night?"

"Coffee," Pam grunted.

Jade grinned and pointed towards the back room. "I've already got a fresh pot on."

"Thanks." Pam stumbled once in her heels before disappearing from sight.

Jade cringed as the sound of breaking glass met her ears. "There goes another coffee cup," she muttered to herself. It wasn't the first and certainly wouldn't be the last. Pam was one of the biggest klutzes she'd ever met. She might be tall and striking in appearance, but the woman had no natural grace.

As she took a sip of her own coffee, the bell attached to the front door jingled, and a very slim woman walked in. She looked almost ethereal, and there was a certain grace to her walk. She was a natural brunette, but beautiful golden highlighted her hair, lighting up her pale face. Normally Jade didn't pay this close attention to her customers, but there was an almost tangible edginess that surrounded this woman. She kept glancing around, and dark half-moons were visible underneath her hazel eyes.

"Can I help you find anything?" Jade smiled at her, hoping to put her at ease.

She shook her head and smiled tightly. "No, I'm just browsing. Thank you."

"Well, let me know if you change your mind." Jade gave her space but cringed when she started trying on scarves. If customers said they didn't want help, Jade usually listened, but this woman clearly needed it. Every time she tried to tie a knot at the nape of her neck, the scarf slipped off her head.

"I know you said you didn't need help, but will you allow me?" She spoke softly and motioned to the woman's hair.

The woman grimaced at her own attempts to fasten her hair in place. She handed the silk scarf to Jade. "Yes, thank you."

Jade quickly and expertly pulled her hair into a low chignon. Then she tri-folded the long scarf and tied it firmly behind the woman's neck.

The woman looked in the mirror and a half smile cracked her tired face. She lightly touched the scarf and gave a brief nod of gratitude. "Thank you. For some reason I can never get these things to stay put."

"Try bobby pins. They work wonders, and you can buy them in the exact color of your hair."

"Thanks. Do you sell sunglasses here too?" The woman glanced around.

Jade pointed towards the register. "Right over here. The Jackie O-style is classic. If you pair these with that scarf, you'll have a timeless Hollywood look."

The woman tried on a few but finally settled on a golden-brown pair of Dior's.

Jade started to ring her up when Pam collapsed on the stool next to the register. "Ugh, those creepy men are back again."

"What are you talking about?"

She motioned towards the front window. "Oh, there were some beefy looking goons hanging around outside this morning. They were trying to hassle me, asking about some woman as I walked to work. I told them to shove off or I'd call the police. That sent them scurrying. I'll get rid of them again." She rolled her eyes and stalked toward the front of the store.

Jade shook her head and gave the total amount to the customer who had paled to an ashen gray. "Are you all right?"

"I've just had a long day shopping." The woman took a slim pocketbook out of her purse and pulled out two bills. When she did, Jade noticed an exquisite ring on her finger.

"That's a very unusual ring. I've never seen anything like it."

The woman glanced down at her hand. "Thanks," she said quickly, then darted a look out the front store window.

Visible tremors shook the woman's entire body, so Jade followed her gaze. Two men had their backs to the store, and one of them was talking on his cell phone. Pam had her hands on her hips as she stood by the door like a guard dog.

The woman tore her eyes from the window and looked back at Jade. "Actually, I've been thinking of getting rid of it. It was a gift from my ex-husband. Would you trade me something for it?"

"You're sure?" The band was white gold or platinum and it held a flat oval shaped stone. Surrounding the stone were intricate carvings of some sort. She wasn't a jewelry connoisseur by any stretch, but it looked like it could be a pearly colored sea shell or some other type of glass in the middle.

"It holds a lot of bad memories. I'm not even sure why I've been holding on to it for this long." She slipped it off her slim finger and held it out to Jade.

"I couldn't. Maybe you should think about this a little longer."

The woman placed it in Jade's hand and closed her own over it. "Please. You obviously like it, and it would make me happy to know that someone else will take joy in it."

Jade wanted to say no, but the woman seemed so desperate to get rid of it. "Okay, but in case you change your mind, you can still come back for it."

Relief washed over the woman's pale face. "Great, now how much do I owe you again?"

Jade shook her head. "Nothing. The ring is payment enough." She normally didn't make trades, but for this piece of jewelry, she'd make an exception.

The woman put the bills back in her wallet and snuck another peek out the window. "Do you have a back door to this place?"

A sudden understanding swept over Jade, and she too glanced once more to the men. They weren't paying any attention to the customers inside, but she got the feeling they were waiting for someone. Probably this woman. "Follow me."

Jade paused at the back door. "Are you sure there isn't more I can do to help you? Can I call someone? My brother-in-law is a cop if you're in some sort of trouble."

The woman shook her head. "Hold on to that ring for a few weeks. That's what you can do for me."

"What?"

"Please, promise me you won't sell it." She clasped Jade's hand tightly.

The raw fear in her voice made it impossible to say no. "Okay. I'll do it."

"Thank you. More than you know."

The back door to the store led to an alley that bordered another side street. Jade watched the woman leave and tried to quell her worry for the stranger's safety. She glanced down at the ring and turned it over in her hand to inspect it further. Thinking she might help the woman further, she rushed down to the end of the alley but she was gone, lost amid a sea of tourists and local shoppers.

CHAPTER SIX

David steered his truck into the garage but kept the door open so he could unload it. In an effort to keep Jade off of his mind he'd decided to paint his home office. He'd vowed to give her one day.

One damn day. That was it.

Then they were talking things out. More than talking if he had any say over it. He'd just been getting started the other night.

He lugged a couple of one gallon cans of paint out of the back of his truck and shut the tailgate. Keeping himself busy was the only option until he talked to her. He'd taken time off work and he didn't want to get involved with anything that might distract him and drag him out of town. Halfway up his stairs, his cell phone rang. His heart sped up, and he fumbled to put the paint cans down at the top of the stairs. When he glanced at the number, he cursed the disappointment that raged through him. He was acting like a fucking teenager with a crush.

Answering his phone, he walked into his office. "Hey, man."

"David. I hear you're back in town for a while," said Colin Sullivan, Jade's brother-in-law.

"Yeah, I'm taking time off from work. Mainly I'm fixing up the house." David got along with Colin, but it was strange for him to be calling.

"We're having a barbeque with some of the guys from work next Saturday around noon. The whole family will be there. I thought you might like to come."

"Sure. I remember where you guys live."

"Great."

There was a prolonged moment of silence, and David was under the distinct impression that the invitation to dinner wasn't the reason for the call. "Is that the only reason you called?"

"Not exactly. Look, if I'm out of line then just say so. I don't know what you did, but you pissed Jade off something *fierce*. Maya met her for lunch today and now all of a sudden she wants me to set Jade up with this guy from work. I'm putting it off out of respect for you." He paused and cleared his throat. "Is there any reason I shouldn't?"

"You know about...?" he trailed off.

Colin snorted. "Of course I know how you feel. So does Maya. I can't believe it's taken you this long to do anything about it."

"She wasn't ready."

"Well, she's ready now, and you need to undo whatever it is that made her so angry."

"She's angry?" That didn't make any sense.

"Oh yeah. About what, I'm not exactly sure."

"You didn't ask Maya about it?"

"Hell no," Colin grunted.

"All right. Thanks for the call, I appreciate it. Oh, about that date—"

Colin cut him off before he could finish. "I know. It's not going to happen."

"Thanks, man. I'll see ya next weekend."

Once they disconnected David draped old sheets over the sparse furniture in his office. While he worked, Colin's words echoed in his brain. He couldn't understand why Jade would be *angry*. It's not as if he'd hurt her or pushed her into doing something she was uncomfortable with.

About halfway through the room, he stopped midstroke. He pulled out his phone and called someone he really didn't want to talk to.

Heather picked up on the second ring. "Hey, baby. Did you change your mind about seeing me while I'm in town?"

Involuntarily, he balled one hand into a fist and tightened his grip on the phone with the other. He tried to keep his annoyance in check. "Listen, did anyone stop by this morning when I was in the shower?"

She laughed in that annoying way of hers that made him envision running his head through a wall just so he wouldn't have to hear her. "Maybe."

"Heather, don't play games with me. Did someone stop by or not?" He couldn't believe he'd ever dated this woman, however brief it had been.

She sighed exaggeratedly. "Yes, some tiny little woman came by. I got rid of her."

That was all he needed to hear. Of course Heather would have insulted Jade and she'd probably answered the door wearing—Oh shit. His heart dropped when he realized what Jade must think of him. "What did she say?" His teeth were clenched so tight he was surprised enamel wasn't shooting out his ears.

"I don't remember. She said she'd talk to you later or something. Is she the reason you don't want to see me? You've *got* to be kidding!"

"I've got to go. Don't come by here again." He disconnected before she could respond.

Now things made sense. Heather was one of the few women he'd dated for longer than a week. He hadn't seen her in over two years, but he'd run into her in the Caribbean on his last job. She'd made it pretty obvious she was still interested. He'd brushed her off, using work as an excuse, but since she was doing a photo shoot on one of the local beaches, she'd stopped by that morning and refused to leave. He'd told her he was taking a shower and that she better be gone by the time he got out. Yet when he returned to the room he found her half-naked, draped across his bed. Under different circumstances he might have taken her up on her offer.

But she wasn't Jade.

If Heather had answered his door looking like that no wonder Jade was pissed. Despite the urge to rush over to Jade's store immediately, he finished up with the room. He was going to talk to her about this at her house, not at work where anyone could overhear. And if he tried to call, he guessed she'd hang up on him. Not that he'd blame her. Tonight there would be no distractions and nowhere for her to go.

CHAPTER SEVEN

Jade turned underneath the shower head and sighed in appreciation. The massaging jet streams pounded against her back, easing some of her tension. For the tenth time tonight she wondered why she'd thought babysitting would be a fun idea. Her young nephews were finally asleep. *After an hour of coaxing.* She'd fixed a simple dinner of grilled cheese sandwiches and milk because that's what they'd wanted. As soon as she put their meals in front of them however, they demanded pancakes. Trying to be the cool aunt, she'd obliged. However, when they pounded their tiny little fists on the table and demanded hot dogs, she put her foot down. They were lucky they were so adorable.

Just as she finished towel drying her hair, the faint sound of the doorbell startled her. At first, she thought she'd imagined it, but when she opened the bathroom door, she heard the distinctive chime again.

"What on earth?" she mumbled. No one ever just stopped by. Especially not after nine o'clock in the evening. She quickly threw on a thick, pink terrycloth robe. The doorbell rang a third time, and she sprinted down

97

the stairs. She didn't want the boys waking up. Not after she'd just gotten them to sleep.

Without bothering to look through the peephole, she slung open the door. David stood there, clasping his hands in front of him. She stared, momentarily speechless, but when he opened his mouth, she shoved the door closed.

Or, she tried to.

She'd almost taken him by surprise, but her slight pause gave him the advantage. In one quick movement, he stuck his brown boot in the way.

"Jade, will you please listen to what I have to say?" Using his shoulder, David pried the door open wider.

It was useless to physically battle him so she stepped back and crossed her arms over her chest. Without shoes or proper clothes, she felt devoid of battle gear. It was as if he'd timed it intentionally when she was at her most vulnerable. "I have *nothing* to say to you."

"Fine. I'll stay out here all night. I won't be quiet either, I can promise you that. I'm sure it will give the neighbors something to talk about." He removed his foot from the door and stared at her expectantly.

She couldn't tell if he was being serious, but she didn't want to take any chances. Lately he'd been full of surprises. "Whatever. You can come in for a minute. But I'm only letting you in so you won't wake up Brian and

Owen with your incessant bell ringing. You should have called first."

"You wouldn't have answered. Wait a minute, *who?*" His eyes narrowed dangerously.

"Who what?"

"Who's here?" He asked through gritted teeth.

"Brian and Owen. Maya's little boys. They're spending the night." She spoke slowly and deliberately, as if talking to a small child. What did he think, she was having an orgy at her house?

"Oh. Of course." His face instantly relaxed.

Instant irritation boiled up inside Jade. He shouldn't feel relief. What she did was none of his business. "What did you think? That I had two men here at once?"

Without waiting for an answer she turned and walked back to the kitchen. Her legs jerked underneath her, but she couldn't do anything about it. She wasn't sure what he was doing here and after she'd seen that woman at his house this morning she didn't even want to look at him.

She grabbed a bottle of water from the fridge in an effort to keep her hands occupied. When she turned around she glared at him, waiting for his answer.

He stood in the entry looking dark, angry, and good enough to eat. "No," he gritted out.

The feral gleam in his eyes should have been enough to silence her. But she was angry, and she wanted to hurt him. "Even if I did have men here, it's none of your business."

A long moment passed in which he watched her, silently. Her breathing was shallow and her heart thumped wildly against her ribcage. The tick of the wall clock and their breathing were the only sounds in the room. He stared at her hungrily, which only served to confuse her more. She'd seen that half-naked woman at his house. Did he require so much sex that one woman a day wasn't enough? She hugged her arms around her body, willing him to disappear. Why wouldn't he just leave her alone?

"Jade, stop. I know exactly what you're thinking so just stop." Without warning he stalked toward her, his steps slow and deliberate, like a wolf honing in on its prey. Her mind and body warred with each other.

"No, I will not stop. You obviously know what I saw, so if I want to entertain an entire fleet of sailors for an all-night orgy, I will. After today, I am officially none of your business. Or your friend." She took perverse pleasure when a shadow of annoyance crossed his dark features.

"That's where you're wrong. You are most definitely my business. You have been for some time now." His voice was low but strong.

She started to refute his words when it registered that he stood only inches away. Coherent speech proved to be an impossible task with him towering above. Not to mention his masculine, taunting scent confused her even more. It twined around her, caressing her like a soft breeze. She shouldn't be feeling desire toward him now. Especially not now when he'd proved himself to be a liar.

"I think we need to talk about a few things."

"What things?" She tried to keep her voice casual and uncaring.

"The woman at my house this morning for starters." His dark eyebrows lifted.

Sucking in a deep breath, she ducked away from him and took a seat on one of the high-backed chairs. She needed space between them so she could think straight. The man was a pro at crowding her personal space. "Fine. Talk."

He wasn't going to let her get away that easily. David followed and sat directly next to her. "Her name is Heather. We went out on a few dates a long time ago. *Years ago.* I ran into her on my last job but brushed her off. She's in town though and just showed up this morning and wouldn't leave. I told her she'd better be gone by the time I got out of the shower. I know what you're thinking, and I don't blame you, but I promise you, I did *not* sleep with her. I wouldn't have slept with someone else right after what we shared." David put his hands on either side of her armrests, caging her in.

She was no farther away from him now than she had been by the sink. Worse, she was now trapped. She should feel relieved by what he'd just told her—and okay, she was. But this meant she needed to face what had happened between them. "It doesn't matter if you slept with her or not. I don't care. What you do, or who you do, is your business." She clasped her hands tightly in her lap to stop the tremors. If she could just get her voice to stop shaking she'd be fine.

"Then why were you so upset when you thought I had?" He spoke softly, his eyes searching.

She tried a nonchalant shrug, although it didn't come off as casual as she'd hoped. Instead, her shoulders sort of jerked. "Because." Great, a one word answer. *She was a regular wordsmith.*

"Because?" The corners of his mouth tugged up slightly, but he was smart enough not to smile.

"I don't know. Okay?" she muttered.

"You don't know? Or you don't want to talk about it right now?" He leaned back a fraction in his chair, giving her room to breathe.

Maybe he'd sensed her panic. Whatever the reason, she was grateful for the space. "Both."

She wasn't sure what to say after that. They stared at each other in silence for several moments, but this time she didn't turn away.

Finally, he broke the silence. "I didn't sleep with her, Jade. She's not you, and I don't want anyone but you."

The truth was there, written across the rugged lines of his face and in his deep eyes. If he said he didn't sleep with her then he didn't. She'd been so angry this morning but she'd known him a long time and she could simply tell he wasn't lying. He'd stood beside her during her darkest hours so she owed him the benefit of the doubt anyway.

Relief and anxiety welled up inside of her in simultaneous waves. She was silently relieved that he hadn't slept with someone else. At the same time, she was horrified by the liberation that poured through her veins. It was like liquid fire it was so potent. "Okay."

"What?"

The uncertainty in his voice tugged at her heart strings. "I said okay. I believe you."

An uncomfortable silence descended on the dimly lit kitchen. She sat ramrod straight on the chair. It was impossible to tear her eyes away from his. What was she supposed to say to him now? Being angry with him had definitely had its advantages. At least then she'd had an excuse to ignore what had happened between them.

"Jade?" David broke the silence.

"Yes?" She kept her straight stance, and her breathing came out in shallow little pants.

"Is there anything else you want to talk about?" She knew what he was referring to, but his dark eyes were unreadable. She really hated that, not being able to read him. If she was embarrassed or nervous, her face lit up like Rudolph's nose. Not David. With the exception of the other night when he'd let his guard down, his face was a virtual mask.

She tried to swallow but her throat was too dry. "I guess there's no way to get around this, is there?"

"No." He shook his head slightly and a wisp of his dark hair fell across his forehead.

She resisted the urge to brush it away. Just the thought of touching him did funny things to her insides. Especially since the last time she'd run her fingers through his hair, he'd been between her legs. "I'm sorry I ran out on you."

"Why did you?" The hurt in his voice was palpable.

"I...got scared. I knew you were going to kiss me."

"I'd already kissed you." The tone of his deep voice was so intimate heat flooded between her legs.

"I know. What you did, what you made me feel was amazing. It was weird though. You were suddenly on top of me and you looked so good and...hungry. It's the only word I can think of. And I knew you were going to kiss me and things would be different between us. I wasn't ready for that."

"And you didn't think things would be different after I'd gone down on you? After I'd tasted your sweet pussy?"

Her face flamed at his blunt words. She'd never imagined he'd say something like that to her. Ever. She struggled to string a few words together. "Did you plan for that to happen?"

"Not exactly that, but yes. Last night I'd planned to make it clear what I wanted from you."

"What *do* you want from me, David?"

"I want to spend every possible second inside of you. I want to make love until neither of us can walk. Morning, noon and night. It's all I think about, woman. I want you so fucking bad I dream about it and wake up panting for you."

The stark honesty of his words was overpowering. That wasn't exactly what she'd been expecting to hear. Okay, that wasn't even in the same ballpark. After last night she'd known he physically wanted her, but this, this was something entirely different. Something in his tone of voice told her his feelings went far beyond physical desire. "How long have you..." She couldn't finish.

"Long enough." His voice was quiet. Distant. As if he were pulling away from her.

"How *long*?"

His dark eyes flashed with pain, and for a second his mask dropped again and she could see inside him. "From the second I met you."

She shook her head, trying to deny it. "Not from the moment..."

The statement hit her like a body blow. His expression told her everything.

"Maybe I should have waited a little longer, but when you said you were dating again, something inside me snapped. I won't sit by and watch you go out with other men."

The tight mask he'd kept in place for so long slipped. It didn't completely fall, but the words tumbling from his mouth were so laced with pain and hope she had no choice. Without thinking about the consequences, and without saying a word, she leaned toward him, unable to focus on anything but his lips.

Beautiful lips. Lips she'd never paid much attention to until recently. Now all she wanted was to feel them against her own. For all of a millisecond, his eyes widened, but he didn't resist.

His kiss was tentative at first, and she could feel the restraint humming through him. Tension from his body flowed straight through to hers as he tested her response. Blood coursed through her veins like burning lava. One of his strong hands cupped her face while his other hand moved around her waist, encircling her. She loved the feel of him holding her.

He pulled her out of her seat so that she stood directly between his open legs. With firm hands, he held her tight as if he were afraid she'd bolt. For how she felt now that wasn't going to happen again.

His tongue gently explored her mouth. With sweet, erotic teasing. She moved closer into his embrace with a sudden need to have her body pressed up against his. She wanted to feel her breasts press up against him.

Wanted that extra contact.

Vague awareness of her state of undress registered when the front of her robe slackened and fell. A cool current of air cascaded over her partially exposed body. She gasped when his hand moved over one of her bare breasts.

She'd never moved so fast physically with anyone but with David it felt different. It *was* different. They already knew everything about each other.

With expert movements, he stroked her nipple. His thumb lazily rolled over the hardening bud.

With each tweak and flick, her vagina clenched. It was like there was an invisible string attached to the bud and the building heat between her legs. She'd thought he might take his time but he was intent to touch and stroke all of her.

She didn't know why she was surprised.

When he'd told her he wouldn't sit by and watch her date other men she'd seen the proprietary look in his eyes and heard it in his voice. He wanted to possess every inch of her and she wanted to let him.

Even thinking it scared her. She'd never thought she'd want another man to touch her this way but the thought of David losing himself inside her felt strangely right.

With all the strength she possessed, she managed to pull her face away from his. "David, do you want to—" Her voice sounded husky and sensual, even to her own ears.

He silenced her with another kiss that sent spirals of pure pleasure shooting down her spine. He also didn't stop what he was doing with his hands. Deftly, he tugged the top half of her robe completely open and pushed it off her shoulders. She'd tried to ask if he wanted to move to the living room—or bedroom—but he was obviously content to do this right under the bright lights of her kitchen.

She shrugged out of it, letting it fall. The belt tied securely around her waist was the only thing keeping the robe from pooling around her feet. He tugged and teased her already swollen lips with a new urgency. No longer was he gentle and sweet.

When he tore his mouth away from hers he began an assault along jaw and neck. He'd no doubt shaved that morning but his facial hair had already begun to grow and it scraped against her skin.

The sensation was wildly sensuous.

A low buzz had started in her ears, and it was all she could do to stand upright. She gripped his shoulders when he dipped his head and started caressing her already sensitive nipple with his tongue. With closed eyes, she arched her back to give him better access. His lips closed over the hardened peak and sucked. The action was harder than she expected and positively erotic.

She dug her nails into his shirt as she held on to the last remnants of reasonable thought. A low moan escaped her lips. How could this be happening with David?

"Jade," he whispered against her moist skin.

The intimate way he said her name sent another rush of warmth between her legs. In her haste to put her robe on earlier, she hadn't bothered with anything else. When his hands eased open the bottom flap of her robe, she let him. She knew what he was about to do and was powerless to stop him. He'd already kissed her there so why stop now.

When his hand covered her bare mound he shuddered. "You're not wearing anything?"

"Didn't have time."

"You should never wear any panties," he murmured against her skin. For some reason the words didn't sound like a suggestion.

The thought of going bare all the time had her nipples tingling.

"You like that thought don't you?" he asked as he switched breasts.

"Yes." How could he talk right now?

When one of his fingers slid between her folds, she tried to crawl on top of him. He just chuckled against her breast and tugged her nipple between his teeth. Not hard but enough that she felt it straight to her toes.

He was doing too many wonderful things to her and it was all she could do to stand up.

She wanted him to finish this. She needed for him to finish. With the exception of the night before it had been so long since she'd had an orgasm not self-induced. Now she felt sex-starved. "More," she urged.

"More what?"

"I don't know."

He ran his tongue around her areola. Slowly. Deliberately. When he'd made a full circle, his head tilted up. His dark eyes latched onto hers. "Tell me what you want."

She didn't know. She just wanted to come. "I want to come."

He made a sound deep in his throat. It wasn't words. Or she didn't think it was because she couldn't understand him.

As he pushed another finger in her he kept his hot gaze on hers. Her mouth parted when he started to move in and out. The rhythm was continuous and steady but she needed more. Just a little more and she'd come.

"Tell me what you want." Definitely a command this time.

That's when she understood. "My clit. Touch it. Please."

Immediately he pressed his thumb against the raw bundle of nerves. She trembled at the contact. As he rubbed over her most sensitive area, she stood up on her toes. She was so turned on she felt as if she could crawl out of her own skin.

The surge of pleasure hit her so fast she hadn't expected it. She dug her fingers into his shoulders as she started climaxing. "David," she whispered his name.

She couldn't let go of her death grip on him as her body trembled and shuddered. Finally she wrapped her arms around his neck and let herself sag against him. He kept his fingers buried inside her as the waves of her orgasm subsided. When he finally withdrew them he looped his arm around her back and pulled her tight against him.

David was her rock, steadying her. Without him, she'd be a crumpled heap on the floor. After a few minutes passed she pulled back to face him but he didn't loosen his grip.

She stared at him in slight astonishment. How had he learned the nuances of her body so quickly? If he could do that with his hands, she knew she was in trouble when they finally made it to the bedroom. At this point it was only a matter of when, not if, they slept together. A line had been crossed, and she wanted more of this and more of him. And she really wanted to give him the same pleasure he'd given her.

An unfathomable expression shrouded his features. Unsure of what to say, she stared right back. For a moment it felt as if they were the only two people in the world.

He started to speak when a muted thud directly above them pulled Jade back to reality. *They weren't alone in the house.*

She took a step back out of his embrace and immediately experienced a strange sense of loss. Heat rushed to her face at her disheveled state. She hurriedly pulled her robe back into place. "I need to check on the boys," she mumbled and fled the kitchen.

The brief escape gave her enough time to think about what had just happened and to try to make sense of it all. He'd made it perfectly clear he didn't want anything casual. Dating was fine for now. However, in the deepest recesses of her heart she was afraid she'd never love another man the way she'd loved Aidan. She'd never voiced those fears to anyone, including Maya.

Some things a woman kept to herself. She didn't want to give half of her heart to someone, but in a way she'd already resigned herself to doing just that. Of course, she hadn't expected to react to David's touch with such intensity either. Even thinking about the way he'd kissed and touched her made her nipples harden underneath the thick terry cloth robe.

When she got upstairs, she found Owen asleep on the bed and Brian half-asleep on the floor.

"Are you okay, sweetie? Did you fall out of bed?" She squatted on the floor next to him and she scooped him up into her arms.

He looked around, bleary eyed and confused. "Don't know," he mumbled. "Where's Owen? Where's brother?"

"He's right here. Come on." She hoisted him up onto the bed, and tucked the covers tightly around his tiny body. Their single beds at home were a lot closer to the ground. She'd forgotten that they weren't used to sleeping in a bed together, and Owen had probably kicked him off.

"Night, Aunt Jade," he spoke so softly she almost didn't hear him over his brother's light breathing.

"Good night." She stayed an extra minute to watch them, and when she was satisfied they were okay she went to her room and stripped out of her robe. Normally, she slept in very little, but she pulled out a long pajama set her mother had given her years ago and threw it on. It was from Victoria's Secret, but it wasn't in the least bit sexy. The flannel pink and yellow button-up set covered everything. Well almost everything. She couldn't exactly hide the outline of her breasts. They might be small, but she was still completely and utterly turned on by what had just happened between her and David, and her nipples gave her away. Heat still pooled between her legs and she tingled everywhere.

When she entered the kitchen, David sat in the same spot she'd left him. A flash of disappointment flickered in his eyes. Presumably because she'd changed.

He cleared his throat. "Is everything okay?"

To her horror, her voice shook when she answered. "Yes. Brian fell out of the bed. They're not used to sleeping together, and I have a suspicion that Owen probably kicked him out of bed. Not intentionally, of course, but he's a kicker. Or so Maya tells me. I probably should have—"

"Jade, you're rambling."

"I know." She sighed and crossed her arms over her chest. "I don't know where we go from here."

She'd thought crossing her arms would give him the signal to back off, but he crossed the short distance between them and pulled her against him. "I know this is happening fast for you. How about I take you out for dinner tomorrow night and we'll take things a little slower?" His voice was soothing and impossibly intimate.

She couldn't fight the heat rushing to her cheeks. The hardness underneath his pants when he held her so close was unmistakable. Fortunately, he didn't seem the least bit bothered. "What time?"

"Six?"

She nodded. The earlier they ate meant the earlier they'd get to do other stuff. She knew it. He knew it. Sex was *so* going to happen tomorrow night. If it hadn't been for her nephews, she'd have let him take her right on the kitchen counter. Something he no doubt knew too.

"All right. I'll see you then. Unless…you want me to stay?" His grin was positively wicked and full of promises. He'd never looked at her like that before and it made her heart stutter.

Yes. Her mind shouted to let him stay. Common sense won out. "I don't think that's a good idea, David." She was surprised by the disappointment that surged through her. She needed to get a mental handle on what was happening between them, but her stomach dropped just the same.

"I figured you'd say that." He brushed a light kiss over her lips before letting himself out.

Long after he'd gone, the feel of his lips on hers lingered. As did his intoxicating male scent. For the first time in years, the only man she thought of when getting into bed that night was David.

CHAPTER EIGHT

"You're in a surprisingly good mood today," Maya said as she shut the back door to her van.

Jade shrugged and smothered a grin. "Why shouldn't I be?"

For now, she wanted to keep the subject of David and herself private. As soon as it was out in the open, she knew her family would bombard her with questions. Since she didn't have answers for those annoying little inquiries about the future, silence was the best option.

"Oh, I don't know. Maybe because yesterday you were ready to claw David's eyes out and now you're practically glowing. What happened in the last few hours? Did you talk to him?" Maya put a hand on her hip and narrowed her eyes.

Jade nodded towards the car window. "I think you might want to get them out of here. It looks like they're ready to tear the vehicle apart."

Both boys were jumping up and down, hitting the ceiling with their heads, even though her sister had strapped them in moments before. Jade didn't bother to hide her grin now.

Maya growled under her breath and turned back around. "Fine, but you're not getting off the hook that easy. I know you're hiding something."

Jade hugged her sister and headed to work. The walk was fuzzy. Trees, cars, and people passed in a blur. Her thoughts were so focused on the previous night she was surprised she hadn't been hit by a car. She couldn't even remember crossing any streets. It was close to noon by the time she made it, just in time to give Pam a break for lunch. Pam was helping a customer, so she secured her purse in the back room and pulled out a few of the new boxes. The bell in the front jingled so she stuck her head out to see if Pam needed help but it was just the woman Pam had been helping, leaving.

"Hey, Jade," Pam said in a very strange singsong voice.

She frowned. "Hey," she said hesitantly. Pam had a mischievous sparkle in her brown eyes that made Jade uneasy.

Pam's megawatt grin widened. "You have a special delivery." She pointed behind the cash register.

A huge arrangement of what appeared to be at least two dozen multicolored tulips stood proudly, blooming in the bright sunlight. She'd seen them on her way in and assumed they were an apology from Pam's ex-boyfriend. "Those aren't for you?"

"Nope. They are most definitely for you. Why don't you read the card?" Pam wiggled her eyebrows.

Jade walked over and pulled out the card.

I don't know what the future holds for us, but I meant everything I said last night. See you tonight. David.

Despite the shortness of the note, her heart stuttered. Flowers were something she hadn't received in years, and something she missed terribly. She occasionally bought them for herself, to brighten up her house. It was touching that he'd sent them, even more so that he remembered tulips were her favorite. The heat from Pam's gaze scorched her face, but she resisted the urge to look up.

"Oh, come on, I already read the card." Pam's statement forced her to make eye contact.

Jade rolled her eyes even though she'd expected Pam to snoop. "Is nothing private around here?"

"Are those from the same David I'm thinking of?"

She tucked the note back in the envelope. "Depends. Who exactly is it you're thinking of?"

"Oh, come on. You know *exactly* who I'm talking about. That dark, brooding, sexy man that comes to visit you every couple weeks. Every time he leaves I have to wipe the drool from my face." Pam leaned on the counter and put her face in her hands.

"You think he's sexy?" Pam was more or less a serial flirter, if that was even a word, and she'd never made a pass at David.

"Oh yeah, but he only has eyes for you, so I've never bothered turning on the charm. Why waste my time?" Pam shrugged.

"How am I the only one who didn't see this?" Jade muttered under her breath.

"Because you weren't ready to see it. You've had blinders on for years. And not just with him."

"Please spare me. You sound like Maya." Jade turned around and started straightening a pile of gauzy blouses.

"Don't ignore me. I want details. What exactly happened last night?" Pam moved to the other side of the display table, right in front of Jade.

"That would be none of your business." Last night had been unexpected, and it's not as if she would tell anyone the intimate details, including her sister.

"I just might have to inform Maya that you received flowers from a certain gentleman then." Pam pivoted on her heel and disappeared into the break room.

"You're a monster. Do you know that?"

A few minutes later Pam was back with a cup of coffee for both of them. She handed one to Jade and pulled out a chair behind the register. "I should tell you that your sister called this morning, and I know she was fishing for information. Not that I can blame her. You're practically glowing. It's so obvious something happened. Lucky for you I'm discreet. You can thank me by buying me lunch since I didn't tell her about the flowers."

"Okay, I take it back. You're not a monster, you're an angel. I'm not ready to tell her or my mother anything just yet." She couldn't handle any questions from the family.

"Oh." Pam's face instantly reddened.

"Oh, what? I don't like that look." Her bubble of elation popped with a single word.

"Your mom stopped by this morning." She held up her hands in defeat.

"Please tell me she didn't see the letter."

"Do you want the truth, or do you want me to tell you she didn't see the letter?" Pam expelled a tiny laugh, laced with guilt. "I'm sorry, I couldn't stop her. I tried to be sneaky and she grabbed it right out of my hands. You know how she is."

She did know, more than she cared to admit. "Fine, let's have it. What did she say?" She inwardly cringed as she waited for the bomb to drop. She could only imagine her mother's reaction.

"Nothing."

"Nothing?" She was nearly thirty and her mom still gave her advice on what types of bras she should be wearing.

"I swear. She gave me this strange, secretive smile, and left. It was really bizarre."

"You're sure? No smart comment?"

Pam shook her head. "Yeah, I was just as surprised."

"You? *I'm* surprised she hasn't called me yet. I wonder what..."

The front door jingled, and they both stopped.

A relatively short man wearing a plain blue suit and even plainer blue tie walked in. Everything about him was non-descript. And he could definitely do with some sun. Intelligent, icy blue eyes were the only thing that would make him memorable.

"Hi, do you need help finding anything today?" Jade asked.

He shook his head in an abrupt manner. "No, but I do have a few questions for you."

"Concerning what?"

His blue eyes narrowed into slits. "Concerning an on-going investigation."

She was under the impression he was being intentionally difficult. Probably to intimidate them for whatever reason. She didn't have time to play twenty questions and she wasn't letting some stranger harass her. After the morning she'd had, she wasn't letting anything ruin her good mood. "Do you feel like expanding on that?"

He pulled out a photograph and stepped toward her. Pam, who'd been by the cash register, walked up behind Jade and peered over her shoulder.

"Have you seen this woman recently?" He held the picture out and waved it under their noses.

Pam nodded then looked at Jade questioningly. "Wasn't she that woman who was in here a few days ago? Didn't she trade a ring or something for a scarf?"

She wanted to tell Pam to be quiet but couldn't. "Maybe." The word came out more abruptly than she'd intended. "I'm sorry. You didn't say who you worked for or what this is even about. Or your *name*. I'd like to see some identification please."

He wasn't with the police department, of that she was certain. For one thing, because of her brother-in-law, she was familiar with most members of the local law enforcement. And for another, his dress wasn't right. She couldn't figure out exactly what it was, but everything about him looked wrong. His shoes were Gucci, she was almost sure of it, but his cheap cotton suit couldn't have cost more than fifty dollars.

The man nodded but retained the same vague expression. He pulled out a badge and shoved it in her general direction. "I'm special agent Keith Celan. I'm with the Drug Enforcement Administration."

"What kind of investigation is this, sir?" Jade kept her tone polite and professional even though her skin crawled being so near him. She stared at his badge, as if it could tell her some secret, then glanced back down at the picture, mainly so she wouldn't have to look into those cold blue eyes. A pregnant pause followed, and at first she wasn't sure he would answer.

After a few moments he sighed. "An agent has gone missing, and we're trying to locate her."

"And this is the agent?" Pam asked.

He nodded and looked directly at Pam. "When was it you said you saw her?"

Pam cleared her throat and shrugged. "I'm not really sure. Jade helped her, so you'd have to ask her. I'm going to put on a pot of coffee. Let me know if you need anything else."

The man might be on an investigation, but he had enough time to leer at Pam as she walked away. Jade clenched her hands into balls at her sides, resisting the urge to smack the look right off his face.

"Your friend said something about a ring?" He refocused his attention on her.

She nodded. "Yes. She wanted to trade a ring for some merchandise."

His eyes narrowed just a fraction. "Do you still have the ring?"

Jade shook her head and tried to appear apologetic. Something in her gut told her not to tell this man anything. He was a snake. "No, I'm sorry. Someone else bought it."

"I'm going to need to see records from both of those sales." He demanded.

"Don't you need a warrant for something like that?" She had no idea what protocol was necessary, but she doubted he could just come into her store and start demanding things.

His blue eyes darkened to storm clouds. "Are you telling me that you are unwilling to assist in a federal investigation?"

She clasped her sweaty palms together. "Don't try to twist my words. I'm simply telling you that I'm not allowing some strange man to dig through my records. For all I know, you're not even with the DEA. That could be a fake badge."

He reached into the inner pocket of his suit, yanked out a business card and handed it to her. "Look, ma'am. I'm sorry for my attitude. This woman, Evelyn, has been missing for a couple weeks and we're desperately trying to find her. She's a good agent."

He practically barred his teeth at her in what she assumed was his sad attempt at a smile. Now he wanted to be nice?

"Then why haven't I seen anything on the news about this?" That woman had been scared of someone, and for all she knew this was the man she was running from. He could be some crazy ex-husband or an investigator sent by the woman's ex.

"We're trying to keep this under wraps. I can't go into further details about the case, but she's undercover and we can't have her picture splashed all over the news."

She still didn't think he was telling the truth, but she also didn't want people traipsing through her store later. So, she decided to give the appearance of relenting. "I can pull out the receipts, but I don't think it will do you any good. The woman who bought the ring paid in cash."

"Are you absolutely sure?"

Jade nodded in affirmation. "Positive. I own this store and I'm here practically every day. If you still want to see the receipts you can come back later after I have a chance to go through them." She said a silent prayer he wouldn't call her bluff.

"No, but thank you for your cooperation. I assume you'll be available if I have any more questions."

"Of course, although I don't think I'll be able to help you."

He started to leave but turned back midway to the front of the store. "Did she say anything about where she was staying or make small talk?"

"No. The only time she really said anything was to ask if we accepted trades."

His flushed face turned a brighter shade of red. "Is that normal?"

"Uh, is what normal?"

"Trades?"

It felt like he was testing her so she shrugged. "No, but I made an exception. The ring was very unique, and I knew it would be easy to sell."

He nodded in acceptance of her reply. "Okay. Please contact me if you see or hear from her again."

"Of course." She gritted her teeth and put on what she hoped was a gracious smile.

Without commenting further, he turned and walked out the front door.

As soon as he had gone, Pam popped her head out from the back room and gave an exaggerated shudder. "Ick."

Jade mirrored her sentiments. "I know. What a creep. That's enough excitement for the day. Let's start opening those new boxes."

* * *

Keith Celan pulled out a cell phone the instant the door to *My Sister's Closet* shut behind him. This wasn't his work cell, but a cheap throw away he'd purchased after arriving in Saint Augustine. Something that couldn't be traced back to him. He dialed one of his contacts at the DEA division in Washington DC.

The man on the other end picked up after only one ring. "Chapman here."

Without bothering to identify himself, he started barking orders. "I need you to pull up everything we have on Jadyn Hadley, also known as Jade." Keith looked around quickly to make sure he wasn't being followed, then ducked down a small, semi-hidden, cobblestone alley. Green and yellow awnings gave him cover from the sun, and above him, a bar blaring Jamaican music from two huge speakers was in full swing. In case he was being tailed, it would be difficult to hear his conversation, even with parabolic microphones.

"That's the owner of that store, *My Sister's Closet*, right?"

"Yes." He had a dossier on all the store owners in downtown Saint Augustine. Rumors had been flying around that Evelyn had been spotted alive a few days ago. She'd been seen in a few of the shops so he'd done his homework on the different owners and their employees. He needed to get to Evelyn before anyone else did.

"Okay. She goes by the name Jade. Her maiden name is Bancroft. She's a widow. Her husband was a US Marshal. He was killed in the line of duty. She has one sister who's married to a local cop. They've got two kids. Her parents are retired. Mom was a teacher, and father owned his own construction company after retiring from professional surfing. He comes from old family money. Jade doesn't have kids. No pets. No boyfriend to date. As far as we know, she doesn't date very often."

That meant she lived alone. Perfect. "Is that all you have on her?" Keith was positive she was hiding something from him and he intended to find out what.

"Just about. She pays her taxes on time. She's runs in a couple half marathons every year for breast cancer. No traffic tickets on file. She's a model citizen. And by the looks of her pictures, she's smoking hot. Why are you so interested in her?"

"I questioned her today about seeing Evelyn and she lied to me."

"How can you be so sure? What reason could she possibly have to lie?"

Keith tried to keep the exasperation out of his voice. "Because I've been in this business for twenty-three years and I know when someone is lying to me. See if you can find some connection between them. I doubt there is, but she still knows something more than she's letting on."

"All right. I'm on it."

"One more thing. You worked with Evelyn right?"

"Uh, yeah. Before she moved down to Miami we worked a few cases together."

"Did she ever wear any jewelry? A ring maybe?"

"Yeah. Actually, she never wore any jewelry except a ring. She once told me that her father gave it to her before he died. Why?"

Keith wasn't about to tell Mark Chapman anything. "It might be important. I'll let you know if it is. Keep me updated if you find out anything else on the Hadley woman."

As soon as they disconnected, Keith made his way to the rental car he'd parked a few blocks away. Once inside he pulled out another burner phone and placed a call.

"Yes?" A quiet, heavily accented voice asked.

"I might have a lead on the missing woman. Can you spare one of your men?"

"What kind of job?"

"Intimidation only."

"Send me the relevant information."

"You'll have it within the hour." Keith disconnected and headed back to the bed and breakfast he was staying at. Jade Hadley *would* tell him what she was hiding. He hoped she wouldn't come to any harm, but if that's what it took then so be it. He was ready to retire and no one would get in his way.

CHAPTER NINE

"See you tomorrow, Pam." Jade waved as she stepped out onto the nearly deserted cobblestone street. The light breeze ruffled her dress and hair as she headed home. A few street lights flipped on and Jade picked up her pace.

David would be at her place to pick her up soon and she still needed to shower and figure out what she was going to wear. Normally, she didn't put much thought into her clothing when she and David got together.

Now things were different. *Very different.*

After looking both ways on King Street, Jade hitched her purse higher on her shoulder and stepped onto the pavement. The sound of screeching tires brought her head up so fast she tripped and snapped a chunk off one of her high heels.

A blue truck barreled down on her. Her heart jumped in her throat. *Move!* Her brain screamed at her but she was frozen. Before she could react, a sudden tug from behind pulled her back to the safety of the sidewalk. She tumbled back with such intensity her leg caught on the curb and her head slammed into the pavement. A slow, burning wildfire of pain spread across her skull. The fading blue sky blurred above her.

"Darling, darling, are you all right? I'm so sorry, I didn't mean for you to fall. I was just trying to pull you to safety."

Carefully, Jade moved her head to the left, in the direction of the familiar voice. Mrs. Katrakis, a local business owner, stared down at her with black, penciled in eyebrows knitted together in concern. Tears welled in the woman's dark eyes and while Jade wanted to tell her not to worry about it, she couldn't muster the strength.

"What happened?" Her voice shook.

Mrs. Katrakis' slightly wrinkled face creased into a tight frown. "That truck tried to run you over, dear. I think he was aiming for you."

She let out a shaky laugh and attempted to sit up. "That's crazy." The guy had obviously been speeding but there was no way it was intentional.

"Here. Let me help you." She was the same height as Jade and at least thirty years older, but she pulled her up with relative ease. "I got most of the license plate, but I couldn't get the last digit. My old eyes aren't what they used to be." She grimaced and smoothed down Jade's now wrinkled dress.

Clumsily, Jade tried to help, but the moment she looked down, a wave of nausea gripped her. Her stomach lurched. Without explaining, she gripped Mrs.

Katrakis' hand and allowed herself to be lead to a stone bench inside the garden of the nearby Episcopal church. The garden was attached to the church right off King Street, and it was far enough away from the foot traffic that Jade had some privacy if she puked.

"Mr. Taylor is calling the police," Mrs. Katrakis informed her a few minutes later. Mr. Taylor ran one of the local Irish restaurants and would have moved the sun if Mrs. Katrakis had asked him to. How he even knew what was going on was a mystery. Some of the other store owners and a group of tourists had gathered outside the courtyard, but she wasn't sure what all the fuss was about.

"That's not necessary. Please, I wasn't paying attention to where I was walking. There's no need for this. I just want to go home."

The older woman patted Jade's arm. "You hit your head pretty hard so you might have a concussion. I don't want you moving around."

She tried to close her eyes, but Mrs. Katrakis shook her shoulders, and she wasn't gentle about it either.

"Don't even think about it, Jade. If you do have a concussion, sleeping is the last thing I'm letting you do," she said in a tone similar to the one Maya used when scolding her boys.

"Please—"

"Don't argue. The ambulance will be here any minute. I made sure Mr. Taylor informed the dispatcher who your brother-in-law is." Mrs. Katrakis winked and patted her hand.

The older woman had known her and Maya since they were kids, and she adored Maya's husband. She was always sending baked goods home with Jade, never forgetting to remind her to share them with Colin and Maya. It's a wonder she hadn't called him personally. Oh hell, maybe she had.

Sirens tore through the air, and the ringing in her head grew. All she wanted to do was curl up into a ball and block out the noise.

"Will you be all right by yourself for a few minutes?" She clasped her hands over Jade's and frowned.

"I'm fine. But will you do me a favor and call my sister? If she hears about this from Colin she'll freak out. Just let her know I'm okay." She fished her new cell phone out of her purse and handed it to her.

"Thank you." Forcing her eyes to stay open, she focused on one of the magnolia trees in the courtyard. The gentle swaying of the leaves and the sweet aroma eased her headache somewhat.

"Jade?" A male voice tore her out of her trance. She turned to find a man wearing an EMT uniform walking through the stone entrance of the garden.

"Yes." She stood up. Her knees jerked underneath her, but she managed to stay on her feet. She recognized the man, but couldn't place from where exactly.

"Hi, it's Peter Tillman. We went to school together." When she didn't respond he half smiled. "Any of that ring a bell?"

She frowned at him. "I think you were a year or two ahead of me. Weren't you in Maya's class?"

He shook his head. "No, I was in between the two of you."

"Sorry, my head is a little fuzzy. Judging by your uniform, I'm guessing you're here to see if I have a concussion?" she asked.

He nodded. "I'm going to ask you some questions that might seem stupid, but I need to determine the severity of your injury."

"Okay, but where is Mrs. Katrakis? She said she'd be right back." The woman still had her phone.

"She's just answering some questions for the police." He pointed in the direction of flashing lights just barely visible through the trees.

"The police?" She was afraid this had blown up into something much worse than it was.

"She said the man who almost hit you sped up instead of slowing down. Do you remember any of that?"

"Yes, maybe, well, not really." The vision of the truck honing in on her was clear, but the only other thing she remembered was her head slamming onto the sidewalk. And if she forgot, she was sure she'd have a splitting headache for hours to remind her.

She winced as she eased back down on the cold bench. When her skin touched the cool stone, an involuntary shiver ran down her spine.

"Here. Take this." Peter pulled off his lightweight wind breaker and put it around her shoulders.

It engulfed her, but when another shiver racked her body, she drew it tighter. It had been warm this morning but Florida weather in the winter was erratic. It felt as if the temperature had dropped ten degrees since then. "Thanks. Shouldn't we be doing this in the ambulance?"

"Normally, yes, but there are a lot of onlookers and I didn't think you'd want everyone staring at you."

"Thanks."

"Do you know where you are?"

"Yes. I'm in a courtyard sitting on a bench." As forewarned, the questions were stupid, but she nodded and answered each one. For the next twenty minutes she answered what felt like a billion questions ranging from what was her age, what day it was, who was the president, and what she had for breakfast. He also tested her balance, coordination, and reflexes.

When he was through with his evaluation, he snapped his notebook shut. "Your balance is a little off, but I think it's safe to say you don't have a concussion. I'm recommending that you take some Tylenol for your headache. Just don't take any headache medicine with aspirin in it, okay?" He stood up and started walking in the direction of the small parking lot off to the side of the church.

Jade followed suit and walked with him. At the exit, she saw that the flashing lights had been deceiving. It had looked like an entire army of officers were beyond the courtyard when there was just one car and one police officer.

"Okay. Nothing with aspirin. I think I can remember that." Her headache was fading and the only pain she really felt was in her upper body. When she'd hit the ground, her shoulders had taken the brunt of the impact. At least she didn't need to go to the hospital. A few bruises as opposed to a broken body, she could deal with any day.

"Do you have anyone to stay with you tonight?"

"Excuse me?" She stumbled in her already broken heels, but he caught her elbow in a protective grip.

He chuckled lightly. "I seriously doubt you have a concussion, but someone needs to wake you up after a few hours to make sure you can wake up."

"Oh. Of course." She was thankful for the semidarkness that hid the flush in her cheeks. Maybe she had hit her head harder than she'd thought.

"Did you think I was inviting myself over?"

"God, I'm so sorry. The question took me off guard. Blame it on my head injury."

"That's okay. One of the officers will want to talk to you, but it shouldn't take too long."

"It won't take any time at all." A deep voice from behind them made her jump.

"David. What are you doing here?" She swiveled and had to catch herself from falling once again.

He stepped out from the shadows of one of the trees. He appeared almost angry, but she couldn't imagine why he would be. She also didn't understand why he was here.

"I'm here to take you home." He answered her unspoken question and his words were clipped.

"How did you know I was even here?" She didn't remember asking Mrs. Katrakis to call him. Or had she? Everything had happened so fast.

"Maya called me. She wanted to make sure you were okay and that Mrs. Katrakis wasn't confused by what had happened. I got down here as fast as I could."

She rubbed the back of her skull and concern flickered across his face. Despite the intense gleam in his eyes, his words were soft. "Are you all right?"

"I'm fine, I just want to get home."

He turned his attention away from her and looked at Peter, his eye's narrowing slightly. "I've already talked to

Officer Morales. They can take her statement tomorrow. Is she free to go?"

Peter nodded. "Yep, she's got a clean bill of health. Although, she will need someone to wake her up at least once tonight to make sure she doesn't have a concussion."

"It's taken care of. I'll be staying over." He moved over to Jade and put a possessive arm around her shoulders.

She started to protest, but the dark look in his eyes stopped whatever she might have been about to say. He might as well have been a dog marking his territory the way he was holding on to her. Mutely, she nodded.

"I'm parked over there." He pointed to the other side of the parking lot, and she noticed his truck for the first time. They started to leave when she remembered she was still wearing Peter's jacket.

"Oh, I almost forgot." She slipped off the windbreaker and handed it to Peter. "Thanks for making everything so easy."

"No problem. And don't forget what I said. Nothing with aspirin in it."

"I promise. It was good seeing you again." She smiled and half waved as she walked away with David.

He was silent the rest of the way to the truck, even when he opened her door and helped her inside. "Thank you for coming to get me. I hadn't even thought far enough ahead about how I'd get home."

"You don't have to thank me for anything, Jade. I just wish I'd known sooner." He kicked the truck into gear and turned out onto the street.

"I couldn't even think straight earlier. I gave my phone to Mrs. Katrakis and told her to call Maya." She sighed and laid her head back on the seat. "You don't have to stay over tonight you know. Peter said I didn't have a concussion."

"Peter, huh? You seem to know him pretty well." His voice had an unmistakable edge.

She opened her eyes and glanced at him. "Is that why you're acting weird?"

He didn't respond, but she could see the whites of his knuckles as he gripped the steering wheel.

"Jealousy doesn't look good look on you, David." She shook her head and immediately regretted it.

"You still didn't answer my question," he growled.

"We went to school together, and if I remember correctly he had a monster crush on Maya. Besides, after last night I wouldn't think you'd be worried about anything anyway." After last night he should know he had nothing to be worried about. She'd been scared of the thought of letting anyone else touch her but with David, everything had been so natural.

"I didn't like the way that guy was looking at you," he muttered.

"Somehow I have a feeling you wouldn't have liked it if he'd been an eighty-year-old man with a walker. David, he was just doing his job."

"I should have been there." He sighed and turned down her street.

Jade reached out and laid a light hand on his leg. "I would have called you immediately, but it's second nature for me to call Maya for anything."

He steered the truck into her driveway and put his truck in park. "I know. When Maya called and said you'd been hurt, I thought... She didn't give me many details except that you'd almost been hit by a car. She wanted to come too, but I told her I'd take care of things. Then when I got there and saw you wearing that guy's jacket..."

When he didn't continue she unsnapped her seatbelt and opened her door. She understood what he was trying to say. "Come on. If we don't get inside soon I'm liable to pass out in your truck."

He reached behind his seat and grabbed a large bag.

She frowned at it. "What's that?"

"An overnight bag." His voice was wry.

"Don't be a smartass, David. I know what it is. It just looks a little..."

"A little what?"

"Big."

"That's because I'm staying over for a few days."

A few days? He couldn't be serious. "I really don't think that's necessary."

"Don't waste any energy arguing because it's happening." He heaved his bag on his shoulder, took her purse from her hands, and headed for the front door.

Once inside he disappeared up the stairs, presumably to put his things up. Jade headed straight for the kitchen. Her headache was fading and even though it was still early she was ready to sleep and medicine would help that happen faster. No sooner had she popped two tablets in her mouth, and David appeared in the doorway.

"Feeling any better?" he asked.

"A little. I think I'm a bit more shaken up than hurt." She took a seat at the center island.

"So what happened? Your sister wasn't very helpful." He followed suit and sat next to her.

"I'm surprised she didn't rush right down there," she said.

"She wanted to, but Colin was still at work and she didn't want to bring the boys down there and have them jumping all over you."

Remembering what had happened the night before in the exact place they now sat, Jade forced herself to focus on the present situation. "Everything happened so quickly. I remember stepping from the curb, a truck barreling down on me, and then being pulled to safety."

"If anything had happened to you..." He shuddered lightly and for a brief moment she saw a side of him he rarely showed to the world. He looked scared. Honest to God afraid.

For her.

Something cinched around her heart but before she could dwell on it, David leaned in slowly. He gave her time to pull back before he covered her mouth with his.

Her breath caught in her throat as their lips touched. With her head already hazy, this only added to her lightheadedness. He gently explored her mouth with his tongue, taking her bottom lip teasingly with his teeth. His lips were soft and gentle. There was nothing fervent about this kiss. He kissed her like a man with all the time in the world.

One strong hand strayed to her hips and he pulled her closer, gently, as if she were made of porcelain. The other hand settled on her cheek, cupping her jaw. All thoughts of out of control trucks and headaches disappeared. Her heart fluttered, and her knees went weak like she was some silly teenage girl. But she was no girl and David definitely wasn't a boy.

With both hands, she grabbed the front of his shirt and clutched the cotton fabric. She swayed slightly toward him, expecting him to pull her tighter. Lord knew she wanted to increase their kiss. Instead, he pulled back, leaving her dazed and even more confused.

"I think that's enough for tonight, sweetheart. You've had a long day. " His voice and his breathing were rough and unsteady.

Sweetheart. She liked the sound of that. A hot sensation pooled between her legs, and she wanted to protest but knew he was right. Her body craved him, but it also craved sleep. Visions of her plush silk comforter danced in her head. "All right. How long will you let me sleep before waking me up?"

He glanced at his watch. "About two hours."

She yawned and stretched. Normally she didn't go to bed until midnight, but her body wasn't giving her much of a choice.

He walked her to her room, and once they were inside, awkwardness settled in the pit of her stomach. With David so close to her bed it took all of her control to say what she needed to say. She'd hoped to have this conversation under different circumstances, but the words needed to be said, especially since things between them had changed. "David, you know how much you mean to me, right?"

His expression was shuttered as he leaned against the door frame. "I don't think I like where this is going."

She took a step forward and grasped both of his hands in hers when she realized he misunderstood her intentions. "No, that's not what I mean. What I mean is, well, I'm not exactly sure what I'm trying to say. It's just that this *thing* with us, I know it's physical—really physical—and I know how much you care for me. What I don't know is how I…I guess what I'm trying to say is that I don't think I'm leading you on, but I'm still unsure of where we're headed." Okay, she'd just talked herself in circles.

"You don't have to explain anything." His arms went around her like steel bands as he gathered her against his chest. "I know this is all new and unexpected. I don't expect you to have all the answers about us right now, and I'm not asking for any."

"Okay." Her voice was muffled when she spoke into his chest.

He murmured something into her hair, but it was impossible to understand. His hands lightly stroked down her spine, and she wished there wasn't quite so much clothing between them. She wanted to feel his naked body against hers but knew it wasn't happening right then. He must have read her thoughts because he dropped a chaste kiss on her forehead before shutting the door behind him.

* * *

Keith paced the floor of the room he'd rented for the week. He'd opted to stay in a bed and breakfast instead of a hotel because it was easier to pay in cash. He'd made it clear to the owner he didn't want to be disturbed, and so far his needs had been granted. Too bad the men he worked with weren't as competent.

He wanted to punch something. Idiots. He was dealing with idiots. Why the man he'd hired had tried to run Jade Hadley down with a truck was beyond his realm of understanding. He needed her intimidated, not killed. Stupid. That's what he got for dealing with small-time drug runners. She probably wasn't intimidated at all. Shaken up but not terrified like he needed her. She wouldn't have any idea that her near miss with death had been intentional.

He needed to locate Evelyn, the last batch of drugs, and the VX gas and he was certain the Hadley woman could help him. Not that he gave a shit about the cocaine or Evelyn for that matter. The VX gas was all that was important. The men he was dealing with weren't patient, and time was quickly evaporating. They'd only give him so much time until he'd be considered a liability. It's not as if they'd told him outright, but he knew how things worked. The Dominicans he'd been helping smuggle the goods were no problem. They were more or less amateurs, and only concerned with the cocaine.

No, the men he worried about were the Syrians. He'd agreed to look the other way and assist in getting VX gas into the country for them via the Dominicans' regular drug-running route. The Dominicans didn't mind helping because they got paid in cash. Now that the merchandise had gone missing, his time was running out.

Beads of sweat rolled down his face. He needed to make *the call*. With a trembling hand, he pulled out his cell phone and held his breath. Maybe no one would answer.

Someone picked up after the second ring. "Tell me you have good news," the foreign voice on the other end was low and menacing.

He swallowed hard. "Not exactly, but I'm closer. I just need a few more days."

Silence greeted him. Keith inwardly cursed. He shouldn't have called tonight. One more day wouldn't have hurt.

"Do I need to send one of my men to help with the problem?"

"No, I have it under control." Keith didn't want to bring in the Syrians. Even though the Dominicans had screwed up with the Hadley woman, he'd rather deal with them. He'd never met the man he was speaking to but knew of his violent reputation. If he sent someone in there would be a bloodbath in Saint Augustine. Keith wanted this mess wrapped up as much as the Syrian but *without* any fanfare. All he wanted to do was retire quietly and without suspicion.

"What about the woman? Has she given you the information we desire?"

He swallowed again. "We don't even know that she knows anything." When the man didn't respond he rushed on. "But if she does I'll get it from her."

"It will take more than intimidation. She needs to be interrogated then eliminated. A woman like that will go to the police."

Keith wanted to deny it but knew the odds were against them. Her brother-in-law was a police officer and her deceased husband had also been in law enforcement. Even if they told her not to go to the police, she would and wouldn't think twice about it. He didn't want the pretty young woman killed, but she was collateral. "Consider it done."

When they disconnected he poured himself another scotch. How had he gotten here? The answer was simple enough. Money. All he'd wanted was to make some extra money before he retired. With a son in college who barely spoke to him and an ex-wife who despised his existence, he didn't have anything to show for his career. It seemed no matter how many criminals and thugs they put away, ten more were there to replace them the next day. The so called war on drugs was a joke. There was no war, just small battles. In the end, the drug dealers would win.

With a sigh, he stood and swayed against the bed. He didn't think he'd had that much to drink, but the half-empty bottle on the dresser said otherwise. "Story of my life," he muttered to himself.

He picked up his phone, then put it back down. He could make the necessary call in the morning. Might as well let Jade Hadley enjoy one more night of freedom.

CHAPTER TEN

*W*hy *was everything moving?* Jade opened her eyes to find David staring at her. "What's going on?" she muttered.

"Just making sure you can wake up." His hand lightly gripped her shoulder.

"Well, I'm awake." She sat up and glared at the clock. *Almost one.* She understood that he needed to wake her up every couple hours but it was still annoying to finally get to sleep only to be jostled awake again. She shoved her covers back and started to get out of bed.

"What are you doing?" He kept his hand on her shoulder.

"Going to the bathroom and I don't need any help."

"Oh, right." He stepped back and let her pass.

Once alone, she splashed her face with cold water then brushed her teeth. She was never going to get much sleep and if she was honest, she wasn't sure she wanted to. The last time David had woke her up she'd known without a doubt she was fine. No headache, no dizziness, nothing.

But she was also turned on. *Annoyingly so.* His close proximity made it worse. She'd been dreaming about him when he'd jostled her this time and it had taken a moment to realize that it had been just that. *A dream.*

She pressed a finger to her lips. They even felt swollen from her imaginary kisses. Jade flipped off the light as she stepped back into her room.

That's when it hit her. David had made a sleeping pallet by the foot of her bed. He was all stretched out looking so good—too good—without a shirt on.

He propped up on his elbows when he saw her. "You okay?"

She shook her head at his worried tone. "You worry way too much. I swear I'm fine… Why are you sleeping on the floor?"

With the limited lighting streaming in from the cracked blinds his expression was hard to read but she could see his frown. "In case something happens I just want to make sure—"

"No, why are you sleeping there when my bed is more than big enough?"

He cleared his throat but didn't move. "That's not a good idea."

She stepped farther into the room and sat down next to him. "Why not? You've already…" Her face flamed as she tried to formulate her words. What was she going to say? *Seen me naked? Tasted me? Given me the most intense orgasm I've had in years? Twice.*

"Already what?" he murmured, his voice seductively low.

She lightly smacked his arm. "You *know* what. This is ridiculous. I didn't realize you were down here earlier or I'd have never let you stay."

He lifted a dark eyebrow. "Let me?"

She nodded. "That's right."

Sighing, he laid back against his pillow. "Jade, just get into bed. Trust me, I've slept in a lot worse conditions than this."

She knew he had but that didn't ease her guilt any. "Last time I checked we were both adults."

"Hmm." He closed his eyes and slid one arm under his head.

She glared at his still form. If he thought he could ignore her he didn't know her as well as he thought. Stretching out next to him, she laid her head on his chest. The second her head touched him, he jerked underneath her.

She smiled against the solid wall of muscle.

"What are you doing?"

"If you sleep on the floor, so do I."

He muttered something incomprehensible then sat up. "I'd forgotten how stubborn you could be." Before she could react he scooped her up and put her on her side of the bed.

When he walked away she started to get out of bed again but he shook his head. "Damn it, give me a chance to get to the other side."

With a scowl on his face he slid in next to her but kept about a foot of space between them.

She turned on her side to face him. "I don't bite."

He refused to make eye contact with her. He stayed on his back, staring at the ceiling. "Go. To. Sleep."

"I'm not tired."

"Jade, you've been through a lot—"

"All I really did was hit my head on the sidewalk. Not exactly *traumatizing*."

"Well I'm tired so good night." He shut his eyes.

She stared at him as she tried to get a handle on her own emotions. She didn't understand why he was shutting her out. Tonight was supposed to have been their official first date. Kind of strange considering he'd seen and kissed almost all of her naked body.

In a way that bothered her. Not because she regretted anything. No, just the opposite. She felt bad because he'd already given her so much—and not just sexually—but he hadn't asked for anything in return.

Scooting closer, she laid her hand across his stomach. He tensed under her touch but didn't open his eyes.

Trailing down farther, she toyed with the edge of his boxers. His stomach muscles clenched.

His breathing became more labored and the already substantial bulge in his boxers grew even bigger. Still didn't open his eyes though.

Keeping her gaze on his face, she grasped the edge of his boxers and just pulled them down.

Now his eyes flew open. They were full of heat, lust...and regret. "Don't start something we can't finish tonight." His voice was strained.

"I do *not* have a concussion." She wasn't going to say it again.

Ignoring the argument she saw on his face, she tore her eyes away and drank her fill of all that hot, hard flesh.

She'd known he'd be well endowed, but good Lord, he was huge. She pushed out a slow breath and stared at him.

David cursed under his breath and attempted to pull his boxers back up but she slapped his hands away. Before he could move she pulled them all the way off then knelt in between his legs.

"Jade." Her name came out like a desperate plea.

"I want to taste you." She wasn't asking.

She sat there, watching him. Waiting. As she did, she grasped his hard length and squeezed. Gently, slowly, she moved upward.

His eyes heated to scorching, molten lava.

That's all the encouragement she needed. She shimmied down a few inches but he wasn't finished. He grasped her hand, the one holding onto him, and held it. "Jade, if you're doing this out of some sense of—"

"I want this. I want you. And I'm not in pain if that's what you're worried about." Her words were barely a whisper. She didn't want to break up the quietness of this moment. She desperately wanted to taste David. To kiss him that way. Everything about the act was so intimate and she wanted to know him on that level.

His lack of argument told her didn't want her to stop either.

She kept her hand firmly around him. His thick length was hot in her hand. Like a warm, steel pipe.

Leaning forward, she shuddered at his straining erection. The sexual tension in the air was so thick it wrapped around her like a shroud.

A drop of pre-come formed at the tip of his cock. Without working up to it, she just licked the pearly drop off. It was somehow sweet and salty at the same time. She sighed in appreciation and he groaned.

"Damn, Jade."

She looked up at him to find him staring at her. His gaze was so hot she felt as if she could actually combust or burst into flames. The look in his eyes held all sorts of dark promises. Promises she really hoped he kept.

It had been years since she'd thought of sex and it was as if all her dormant urges had rushed to the surface at once. She'd never felt so hungry. So driven with the desire to give pleasure to someone else.

"Suck me." His words—words she'd never thought to hear from him—sent a ribbon of desire curling through her, straight to her toes.

She planned to. Grasping the base of his erection, she started at the top. She kissed and lightly raked her teeth over him. So light she barely touched him.

That got a reaction. His hips jerked and he murmured words and phrases that had her face flaming. He was too big to fully take in her mouth so she held onto the base and sucked him into her mouth as far as she could go.

His fingers threaded through her hair. He held onto her skull in a dominating grip but he wasn't holding her tight. Just enough to let her know he enjoyed it.

She smiled against his hard length as she sucked him into her mouth again. When she'd been thinking about dating again all she'd done was focus on the negatives. Having to touch and kiss another man had been fears and something like this had been seen as a chore. Now she wondered how she'd ever thought in those terms.

She felt powerful, sexual and utterly feminine taking him like this. Her vagina clenched with need but this was about him. He'd already given so much to her and she'd be damned if she couldn't give him pleasure.

As she moved up and down she tasted more of his saltiness. With each stroke his breathing became louder and more labored.

"Oh yeah, sweetheart." Most of his words were a jumble but she understood those.

His balls had pulled up impossibly tight. She'd already gripped them in her other hand so she knew he was close. Using her nails she lightly teased and tugged his sac.

When she did his entire body jolted.

"I'm about to come." He was giving her the opportunity to pull back but there was no way she would.

She didn't want to. Increasing her grip on him she squeezed a little harder and worked him where her mouth wouldn't reach.

In sync, her mouth and hand worked him up and down. Over and over.

Finally it was too much. His fingers tangled deeper into her hair as he shouted. His semen hit the back of her throat in long, hot spurts.

As she swallowed he moved harder, faster, spilling a seemingly endless amount of his seed into her mouth. His taste washed over her tongue and she knew it was something she'd never forget. The essence was all him. All David.

It didn't matter that she hadn't climaxed. Her nipples and vagina tingled knowing she'd given him what he'd given her the day before. Giving him that release gave her more than just a sense of power. It made her happy.

Finally she lifted her head. His eyes were half-closed, heavy lidded with pleasure. He blindly reached for her and hooked his hands under her arms. He lifted her up so that she was sprawled on top of him.

His hands tangled into her hair again in another dominating grip as he ate at her mouth. His tongue, sweet and demanding at the same time invaded her. He nipped and teased her, tugging her bottom lip hungrily.

Finally he pulled back and she sucked in a breath. "Tomorrow..." He didn't finish because he didn't have to.

She knew what tomorrow would bring. His heart pounded erratically against his chest with such intensity she could feel it against her own. And she returned the sentiment. Inside she felt wild and a little out of control.

Tomorrow there would be no barriers between them. No clothes. No crazy people in trucks trying to run her over. Nothing. The timing wasn't right now. She didn't know how she knew. She just did.

Part of her felt as if they'd been building up to this moment forever. And another part of her, the part that felt guilty for feeling so much pleasure with a man who wasn't her husband, wondered why the hell she thought she deserved a second chance at happiness.

CHAPTER ELEVEN

"Jade, stop worrying. Everything is running smoothly. Rosa is great with the customers so there's no need for you to be here. More to the point, if I had a man as hot as David waiting on me hand and foot I can *guarantee* work is the last place I'd be." Pam motioned to where David stood just outside the front window. Jade followed her gaze. As if he knew they were talking about him, he glanced up from talking on the phone and smiled at Jade.

An intimate, knowing smile that only lovers share. Somehow when he looked at her she felt as if he could see inside her, and knew exactly what she was thinking. Her desires, her wants, everything.

"Whatever, Pam," she mumbled. Even if David hadn't sent flowers the other day, he'd made no secret of his feelings for her. The moment they'd entered the store he'd been her shadow, never letting his hand leave the small of her back. Until she'd been forced to kick him out. She could deal with his close proximity, but when he'd practically growled at one of her regular customers, who was only attempting to ask her a question about sizing, she'd ordered him out. Apparently, even sixty-year-old men weren't safe from David.

"I'm going to break down the empty boxes in the back, then I guess I'll clear out."

Even though she was loath to admit it, Pam was right. They didn't need her here. She'd realized it about two minutes after her arrival. She hadn't really been worried about the store. Pam was more than competent. No, she'd needed to get out from under David's watchful eyes. Every time he looked at her, she remembered what had happened in her kitchen and her bedroom, and she wanted more of it. So much so that she'd been distracted to the point of using her shampoo as body wash this morning and body wash in her hair.

When he'd woken her, his eyes hadn't been able to hide what he wanted. They'd blazed with need. For her. What terrified her most was that his eyes mirrored her heart. She hadn't expected to have such a strong physical attraction to anyone. Just a week ago, she'd been contemplating dating again. Now she was contemplating having sex with David. Instead of feeling weird by the idea, she embraced it. Well, her hormones did. Her head, however, was a confused mess.

Shaking her head, she shoved open the side exit door that led to the alley with a quick thrust of her hips. Her nose curled up. The overpowering stench of garbage and rotting food assaulted her in waves. She couldn't prove it without digging through the trash, but she had a sneaking suspicion the new Italian restaurant a few doors down was using her dumpster when they ran out of room in their own. Neither she nor Mrs. Katrakis discarded anything other than cardboard. Holding her breath, she opened the side of the container and blindly threw the boxes in.

A shuffling sound from behind alerted her that she wasn't alone anymore. The hair on the back of her neck stood up, but before she had a chance to move or even think, something cold, metal and sharp bit into her neck.

"Scream and you die," a young, accented, male voice whispered in her ear as he pressed his body up against hers.

She froze and fought the bile rising in her throat. The man holding her was fully erect. This couldn't be happening to her. Not with David so close. Her heartbeat seemed to slow down, as did everything around her. Only seconds before, the sound of laughing tourists beyond the eight-foot wall almost drowned out the blasting music from across the street. Now she heard nothing. Nothing except the roar of blood in her ears and a strange man's shallow breathing.

The man spoke again. "Nod if you understand."

Unable to speak, her head jerked up once and something warm trickled down her neck. Blood. He must have cut her. Strange that she couldn't feel any pain.

"We're going to take a little walk to the end of the alley, and you will not fight me. One wrong move and I shove this Ka-Bar into your stomach and watch you bleed out."

Her legs twitched underneath her, but somehow she managed to move forward. The alley next to her store was blocked from the east and south by a thick coquina limestone wall. Only a small opening to the west led to a cobblestone street. Unlike San Marco Avenue, there was little foot traffic where he was taking her.

She needed to think. Going along with him guaranteed her certain death. *Or worse.* Her heart pumped loudly in her ears, her limbs felt detached from her body, but somehow she found her voice. "What do you want with me?"

"I want to know where that ring is." He shoved her toward the exit when she tried to turn around.

What was he talking about? She wanted to see his face, but she also needed to keep him talking. If he was talking, he wouldn't be busy slicing her up. "What ring?"

He yanked her tight against his body. His words were clipped and flat. "Don't be stupid. The woman in your store the other day. She give you a ring. I want to know where it is."

English wasn't his first language. She filed that bit of information away in case she needed to remember it later.

"How do I know you won't kill me when I give it to you?" He obviously knew about the ring, which left Jade with a dozen questions. Chances were he'd know if she lied.

"You don't. But if you tell truth, I won't cut you into pieces. Your death will be quick. I give my word."

Gee thanks, asshole. She gritted her teeth. "It's in my safe."

"Where?" He applied more pressure to her neck as if she weren't already terrified.

"My store." She motioned with her hand, afraid to make any sudden or wild movements. The last thing she needed was for him to get jumpy and *accidentally* stab her.

He met her with silence. After what felt like an eternity, although was probably only a few seconds, he finally spoke again. "Fine. You come with me until it closes. Then we come back and you get what I want."

She swallowed hard as beads of sweat streamed down her face. He moved the knife away from her neck and shoved her again. Just as he did, she heard a click. It was so faint she might not have heard it, but it was a very distinctive click. One she'd heard many times thanks to being married to a US Marshal. She didn't think. She just reacted. She threw her body against the concrete, ignoring the gravel and stone piercing her palms and elbows.

An explosion sounded above her. Before she had a chance to scream or freak out, David was there. All around her. Holding her. Comforting her.

"Jade? Are you all right? Answer me. Did he hurt you?" David dusted her off as if she were a porcelain doll and turned her around in a full circle, inspecting every inch of her.

Her entire body shook. She didn't know if she was all right. She still didn't know what had just happened. She made the mistake of glancing toward the fallen body. A young man probably no older than nineteen with perfect ebony skin lay in a pool of expanding crimson. Bile rose in her throat and she forced herself to turn away. Something pungent, probably the dumpster, accosted her senses and she swayed into David's chest. He murmured soothing sounds into her hair.

Pam burst through the heavy metal door, causing Jade to jerk in David's arms and push away.

"Oh my God! What happened? We heard shots inside..." Pam stopped mid-sentence and her hand flew to her throat.

The ricocheting of the door against the wall caused Jade to cringe. She didn't know what to tell Pam or what to do.

David started shouting orders. "Call the police and ask for Collin Sullivan. Shut down the store. When the police get here you're not going to be able to help customers if you're answering questions." When Pam simply stood there David added, "Now!"

Wide-eyed and trembling, Pam hurried back into the store.

"Let's get you inside." David put a protective arm around Jade and steered her into the break room.

She sat at the square cherry wood table and picked at some dried drops of green paint as David pulled out a Diet Coke from the mini fridge. She watched it pop and fizz when he poured it over ice. He held out the glass to her, but it took a moment to grasp he meant for her to take it. Thankfully, her arms cooperated with her brain.

After a few refreshing sips, the mist in her brain semi lifted, and she found her voice. "Why did you have a gun?"

He shrugged as he placed a napkin over her neck.

"I'm always armed."

That was news to her. She wanted to push a little more about that, but before she could, he started in with the questions. "Are you hurt? Physically, I mean besides your neck and hands?"

"I don't think so." She held the small cloth in place and looked down at her body. Her clothing was rumpled, and her palms were raw, but she was alive. *Somehow* she was alive. Thanks to David. Later she would ask him what exactly had happened out there, but now she needed to tell him something more important.

He asked another question before she could speak. "How did you know to duck?"

If he kept grilling her, she'd never get her thoughts in order. "I heard the click of your gun. I wasn't even sure if it was you. I hoped and prayed it was since I assumed he only had a knife, but I thought maybe it was him and he was about to shoot me in the back of the head. Aidan took me to the shooting range a lot when he was alive, and I recognized the sound immediately. Instinct and adrenaline kicked in. I didn't even really think, I just reacted."

"I'm glad you did. I had the shot, but with you out of the way, I didn't flinch."

"He asked about the ring," she blurted out before he could ask another question.

With the back of his palm he felt her forehead. "What ring, honey?"

She moistened her lips. "The other day a woman came into the store and wanted to trade a ring for some accessories. Normally I don't make trades, but she seemed so desperate." As quick as humanly possible, she explained about the strange men waiting outside her store that day and her promise to keep the ring safe for the woman.

"Then this DEA agent—or I guess he was—came in the next day and was asking all sorts of questions about her. He shoved her picture in my face and told me she was missing. I couldn't give him anything useful because I don't know anything about her. I didn't even know her name until he told me. And that's assuming he was telling the truth."

"Did he ask you about this ring too?"

She nodded. "The only reason it got brought up is because Pam mentioned it. But I wasn't exactly honest with him. I told him I sold the ring."

His brows knitted together.

"I didn't trust him. Something about him just seemed...off. I can't explain it."

He sucked in a deep breath. "Not telling him probably saved your life. Whoever that man is, he isn't a DEA agent, and if he is, then I can guarantee he's dirty. No one else knew about the ring, so it's more than probable he sent that man after you. It's the only thing that makes any semblance of sense."

She pulled the napkin away from her neck and crumpled it into a tight ball. "First I almost get run over yesterday, then this craziness happens. I should have listened to you and stayed home this morning."

A police siren sounded in the distance and a sigh welled in her chest. More police again. The reality of what could have happened if David hadn't been there sent a tremor skittering over her skin.

"That should be Colin," she said, mainly to break the silence.

David nodded. "Don't tell anyone else about the ring except Colin."

"What? Why?"

"The dead man in your alley isn't some run of the mill mugger. That much we know."

"Uh, how do 'we' know that?"

He faltered and she could tell he was trying to hide something.

"I don't like that look."

He cleared his throat. "Ah, the spider tattoo on his neck is a Dominican gang symbol. A well known gang heavily into drugs, prostitution, and a lot of other things you don't even want to imagine."

"Why can't I tell the police then?"

He shook his head. "Evidence goes missing more often than people think. If you turn the ring over now, you run the risk of never seeing it again. We'll let Colin know and see what he says. Do you remember the DEA agent's name?"

She nodded. "He gave me his card. I tossed it in the cash register. It's probably still there." Her head swam with a million questions, but David's expression told her not to bother. He was on a mission of some sort. Not that she was complaining. Her insides shook, and without him, she'd be wreck. Actually, she'd probably be dead, but that was something she wouldn't allow herself to dwell on. Not yet. Not until she was alone.

"Stay here, I'm going to go get that card. Once I have Colin alone I'll tell him about the ring."

She opened her mouth to protest, but he silenced her with a look. "My main concern is getting you out of here alive, and until I know you're safe, I'm not willing to trust anyone. Including the local police."

David shut the door to the break room behind him. When he entered the store, he wasn't surprised to see it had emptied out. Pam and Rosa sat huddled behind the cash register on two stools.

"The place was empty when we heard the shots so I locked the front door like you said," Pam said.

"Good. Jade told me she put a business card in the cash register. Would you mind getting it for me?"

She hopped up and fumbled around with the silver key. "Of course. How is Jade?"

"She'll be all right once I get her out of here." He took the card from Pam's hand, then slipped it into his back pocket. "The police should be here any minute. Why don't you go check on Jade and make a fresh pot of coffee?"

Pam and the new employee quickly shuffled out of his way, leaving him in silence. As soon as they were out of ear shot, he called his business partner, Nick.

Nick picked up on the second ring. "Hey, man, what's going on?"

He pulled the card back out to read off the necessary information. "Listen, I need you to run a name for me. Keith Celan. He's supposedly with the DEA in Miami. Find out anything you can about him and get back to me immediately."

"All right, I've got a few contacts with them, although not in the Miami area. I'll see what I can come up with. Not that it matters, but what's going on? Is everything all right?"

"No, but I don't have time to explain. Call me with whatever you find out. I know it may take a while but I don't care how late you call."

As soon as they disconnected, a sharp rap on the French doors alerted him. He glanced up to find Colin Sullivan and another man he didn't recognize standing behind the glass. He opened the door and immediately locked it behind them.

"How's Jade?" Colin asked.

"She's holding up. Pam's in the back with her."

Colin nodded. "I figured you wouldn't leave her alone. Since Pam told the dispatcher where the body was I sent a team around back to section off the scene. The uniforms will keep the area secure until we're through here. First I have a few questions."

David leaned against the glass case that supported the cash register. "Go ahead."

He didn't miss the covert look Colin gave his partner who immediately disappeared towards the back room. David lifted his eyebrows knowingly. "Keeping us separated huh?"

"Look man, I've got to follow procedure. You know how it is. Where's your weapon?"

David withdrew it from his ankle holster, unloaded it, and handed it to Colin. Next he pulled out his concealed weapons permit. "You going to take me in?"

"You need to make an official statement downtown but... First, why don't you just go ahead and give me a rundown of what happened. All I know so far is that there's a dead man in the alley."

"Jade wanted to come by the store this morning just to check on things. I was out front on my phone, and when I came back inside Pam told me Jade was ready to leave after she took out the trash. So I headed to the back to help her out."

He tried to quell the shudder that snaked through him. The vision of that man with a knife to Jade's neck was too fresh. He needed to get her out of there, not answer a bunch of questions. "When I opened the door a man had a knife to Jade's throat. I couldn't hear what he was saying, but he was pushing her towards the end of the alley. It was obvious he wasn't going to do whatever it was he planned to do here. I didn't think about it. I knew if I alerted him, the chances of Jade being killed jumped about ninety percent. I took the shot. He died. That pretty much sums it up." He shrugged.

That brief description might sum up the actual events, but it didn't begin to cover what he was experiencing inside. When he'd seen Jade with a knife against her soft, delicate flesh he'd seen red. Even though he knew she was safe in the break room with Pam, the most primal side of him wanted to kill that guy all over again. And again and again. He knew Colin couldn't see his inner turmoil, but it raged beneath the surface just the same. He'd never lost his cool, not even when he was a SEAL. Especially not when he was a SEAL. He had a reputation for keeping a level head. That's one of the reasons he was so good at what he did now. Nothing could have prepared him for the hollow feeling in his gut at the thought of losing Jade. God couldn't be that cruel. Not now. Not when they finally had a shot together.

"Have you ever seen the man before?" Colin asked.

He shook his head. "No, but I recognized one of his tattoos."

"Prison tat?" Colin asked.

"Worse. Gang symbol of *Los Diablos Negros.*" The Black Devils. David didn't add anything, he wanted the name to sink in.

Colin's brows drew together curiously, but he jotted down everything. "Nothing should surprise me anymore," he muttered under his breath. "I haven't dealt with them since I moved from Miami."

An attack of this nature in the middle of the day, and in the middle of Saint Augustine's tourist district no less, was out of the ordinary to say the least. But a member of an infamous gang making a move on someone like Jade was something else entirely. "There's more, but this has to be off the record."

Colin put his pen down and looked up. "I can't withhold anything if it's important to this case."

Inwardly David groaned. Maybe he should have kept his mouth shut. "Not permanently, just for right now. Jade's safety depends on it." Without losing any of the important details he rapidly filled Colin in on everything from the supposed DEA agent's questions and what Jade's attacker had said before he died.

When he finished Colin was silent. He just tapped his pen against his jaw. Finally he spoke. "Where exactly is this ring?"

David opened his mouth to answer then realized he had no clue. "Shit. I didn't even think to ask."

"I'm going to send a patrolman over to Jade's house."

David started to interrupt, thinking he was sending someone to search for the ring, but Colin held out a hand to silence him. "Hear me out. I'm not going to put this in my report. *Yet.* If the man who attacked Jade is...was in this gang you mentioned, then I have enough reason to send someone over to her place without any further details. Next, I'm going to check up on this DEA agent. If I find out anything significant, then I'm going to have to seize the ring as evidence."

David nodded. "Fine, that's fair."

"I assume Jade will be staying with you?" Colin asked.

"I'm not letting her out of my sight."

CHAPTER TWELVE

David pushed open the guest room door and winced as it creaked and groaned. He sighed in relief when Jade didn't stir. Wisps of honey brown hair fell across her high, exotic cheeks. A few streams of light filtered through, but since it was still daylight, he'd pulled the wooden slat blinds as tight as they would go, blocking out most of the sun. He'd also tucked an extra throw blanket around her to help her sleep better. Not that it really mattered. Once they'd arrived back at his place he'd practically had to carry her up the stairs. She wouldn't be waking up anytime soon. For that, he was grateful.

Luckily she hadn't gone into shock but the stress had taken its toll on her. Often tears or sleep were the only outlet for the kind of shock she'd been dealt.

A vibration from his pocket jarred him back to reality. He didn't recognize the number on the screen, but answered as he stepped back into the hall. "Hello?"

"David." It was Colin.

In the background, David could hear multiple phones ringing and what sounded like hundreds of people talking at once. A woman yelled obscenities. "Where are you?"

Colin grunted. "Where else? I'm at the station, and I've got news."

"Good." David descended the stairs and headed for the kitchen. On the off chance Jade woke up he wasn't sure he wanted her to hear this.

"We discovered a lot more than we originally bargained for. I ran the dead guy's fingerprints and got a hit faster than I'd expected. A lot faster. Within minutes of running his prints, I received calls from the DEA and Homeland Security. Both of them were bitching and moaning wanting to know why I had him in custody. When I told them he was dead the fuckers tried to clam up."

No surprise there. Everything was always such a pissing match. "How does that tie in with Jade?"

"I'm getting there. Most of his contacts were criminals and gang members, and he was under surveillance by the DEA and Homeland Security for dealing with a suspected group of terrorists."

"That's some shoddy fucking surveillance." David struggled to rein in his anger. If they'd been doing their jobs properly Jade wouldn't have been such an easy target.

"Don't get me started. I didn't get much out of Homeland Security, but I have a few friends with the DEA in

Miami so I put out some feelers and mentioned the name Keith Celan. As soon as I did that, I was routed right through to the director. We're not exactly friends, but I'm on a semi first name basis with Alan Costa."

David nodded even though Colin couldn't see him. "I've heard the name before. How do you know him?"

"Before I moved here I worked undercover in Miami. Sometimes we teamed up with the DEA. I've only spoken to him in passing, but for what it's worth, I trust him. Costa said Celan has been under suspicion of treason for the past year, but until recently they couldn't pin anything on him. Two days ago he went missing, which means one of two things. Either he's dead, which I doubt, or he knows they're on to him and has gone underground. I'm betting on the latter."

"Me too," David muttered. Celan had probably been the one to order the attack on Jade. The man had to be desperate, which would explain the attempt to kidnap Jade in broad daylight. "How does this connect to Jade and the ring?"

"I'm still not sure about the ring, but it sounds like the woman Jade spoke to *is* a missing agent. Costa wouldn't tell me much, but she went missing a little over a month ago along with a huge batch of drugs and VX gas. My guess is Celan wants to find the woman and the drugs, cash out, and retire somewhere warm. Did Jade tell you where the ring is?"

David laughed without mirth. "It was in her purse."

"You kidding me?"

"She threw it in there yesterday, but after she was almost run down she forgot about it. It's currently in my safe." Not just any safe. He had a custom made, high-tech digital lock safe that was a scaled down version of those used in jewelry stores. Not impenetrable but not easy for a smash and grab either.

"Good, keep it there for now. I still don't know what it has to do with anything and neither does Costa, but he wants it. I'm sending someone over to pick it up to-night...shit, hold on."

David could hear muffled voices, then Colin yell "Shit!" again.

A second later Colin came back on the line. "I've got to go; Jade's house has just been broken into. I'll call you when I find out more."

"What—?"

The line disconnected.

David set the phone down on the granite kitchen counter. Before making any decisions about what to tell Jade, he popped the top to his Heineken and took a swig. He rarely drank, but the past few days events warranted it. On top of trying to keep Jade safe, he was still trying to come to terms that she returned his feelings, physical-ly at least.

And after last night...His entire body tightened as he thought about it. Seeing the honey caramel curtain of her hair draping over him as she sucked him. That had erased all his previous fantasies. Now his visions would be replaced with the reality.

Jade shoved the heavy quilted comforter off her body and rolled out of the bed. She ran a hand through her rumpled hair and glanced over at the digital clock on the small dresser. She groaned. Eight o'clock. How could she have slept so long and still be tired? It was as if she'd been run over with a truck. She gazed at the bed longingly but thought better of it. David had already let her know that she wasn't going to be staying at home until this whole mess cleared up. Since she had no other clothing with her she needed to call her sister and pick up a few things.

Delicious smells wafted from the kitchen. She paused in the doorway as her breath caught. With his back to her, David stood at the stove, humming a familiar Jimmy Buffet song as he sautéed whatever it was that was making her mouth water. The food wasn't the only thing making her mouth water. David wore cut-off khakis that showed off his tanned, muscular legs, a form fitting T-shirt that did nothing to conceal his broad frame, and a pair of beat up Reefs. She wanted to run her hands up his back and savor the feel of all that strength.

She'd always been a sucker for the surfer types. Not only was he sweet and good looking, but he cooked too. It was hard for her to believe she'd been so blind and that some other woman hadn't scooped him up in the past few years. Her throat constricted at the thought. What if...?

"What do you want to drink?" David asked without turning around.

Startled out of her trance, she stepped onto the cool tile floor and went directly for the refrigerator. "I'll just grab a bottle of water and some Tylenol. How did you even know I was here?"

He half turned and pointed upwards. "The stairs creak. Not to mention your scent."

Her eyes widened and her expression must have been one of horror because he just laughed. "I didn't you say you smelled, I said 'your scent'. It's something tropical, and it's been driving me crazy for years."

"Oh... Good crazy?"

"Very good," he murmured as he turned back to the stove.

Ignoring the butterflies in her stomach, she moved closer and peered over his shoulder, mainly so she could feel his body against hers. Her nipples hardened as she brushed against him and she had to bite back a sigh of pleasure. "What are you cooking?"

"Nothing fancy, just chicken teriyaki stir-fry. Do you think you'll be able to eat anything?"

As if on cue, her stomach growled. "I think so. Do you need help with anything?"

"You can set out a couple plates and silverware, but other than that I don't want you doing anything. Also, I don't know another way to tell you this but someone broke into your house."

All earlier hunger pains evaporated. "What? When?"

He moved the simmering wok onto one of the back burners and twisted the knob off before turning to look at her. His expression softened. "Colin called me a few hours ago. I still don't know any of the details or I'd give them to you. I'm just waiting on the phone to ring."

She didn't say anything. Instead, she took a seat at the whitewashed antique kitchen table and traced her fingers along the distressed surface. Chewing on her bottom lip, she tried to rein in the overwhelming emotions battering against her skull. She'd been almost killed twice in the same week, and now someone had broken into her house. *Her house.* Touched her stuff. Maybe she should have stayed in bed.

"Jade?" David's voice broke into her thoughts.

"What?" Her eyes focused on his concerned face, and she realized he must have said her name more than once.

"I asked if you were all right."

She nodded and pushed a piece of chicken across her plate. "I'm fine, but I think I lost my appetite."

"I understand, but you need to get something in you," he said quietly as he scooped large servings of the stir fry onto each of their plates.

Something or someone? For some reason his words sounded subtly sensuous. She doubted he meant anything by it, but she couldn't stop the rush of heat that warmed her cheeks. He took a seat directly across from her, and she saw realization and a trace of amusement in his eyes. She hated that she was so transparent.

"I've always heard bad things come in threes," she said as she speared two small pieces of chicken and a broccoli floret.

His lips curled into a half-smile. "I guess that means you're out of the woods then."

"Maybe. What if both attempts on my life count as only one bad thing? That means there's one more bad thing just waiting to happen. The way things have been going, I wouldn't be surprised if a plane fell out of the sky and landed on your house. It's probably not safe for you to be in a hundred mile radius of me." The thought of something happening to him because of her made her sick.

"You're worth it." He put his fork down. His voice was low and heated.

She averted her gaze to her plate and shoved another bite in her mouth. She couldn't deal with someone trying to kill her *and* David looking at her like he wanted to take her right on the kitchen table. That was just too much.

"Jade, I—"

A shrill blast from the portable phone caused Jade to jump.

"That might be Colin." Anticipation and terror forked through her body in equal measures as David answered the phone.

He gave her a slight nod so she knew it was her brother-in-law on the other end. For the next twenty minutes, she listened to half of a conversation while staring at the minute hand of the oversized, mahogany wall clock.

"Thanks for calling, Colin, I'll fill Jade in on everything," David finally said.

Jade pushed her chair back and stood up. "Well?"

He gave her a wry smile. "You can sit back down, this will take a few minutes."

"I'd rather stand, thank you." She crossed her arms over her chest, daring him to challenge her.

He opened his mouth to protest, then shook his head. "One of the patrol cops caught a man breaking in to your house, and he had no problem talking."

"Seriously?" Jade watched criminal shows occasionally and never understood when suspects caved so easily. It just didn't seem feasible in the real world.

"But only because he wants amnesty. His wife just had a baby, and apparently, having a daughter has changed him. His only demand is that he and his family are put into protective custody."

Jade frowned. "In return for what?"

"Information. Lots of information. He admits that he's in the same gang as the man who tried to kill you. For years they were pretty low level, basically nothing more than street thugs. Then they infiltrated Miami, Orlando, and Tampa. Just recently they started using Saint Augustine as an entry point to run drugs, mainly cocaine."

"That's insane." She'd grown up there and hadn't known anyone who'd actually used hard drugs until going away to college. Even then, marijuana was usually the drug of choice.

David nodded, his expression grim. "My sentiments exactly. According to your brother-in-law they've been under surveillance by the DEA and Homeland Security for quite some time, so I wouldn't worry too much about them making Saint Augustine a permanent home."

"That doesn't explain why he broke into my house."

"He was under orders to search for the ring. Two men were sent out; one to kidnap you and extract the location of the ring, the other to ransack your house in case you lied."

"What about the man who came into my store claiming to be a DEA agent?" she asked.

"He is, or was, a DEA agent. He fell off the radar two days ago."

"Fell off what?"

"He's gone missing, although he's been under surveillance for the past year on suspicion of treason. They haven't been able to nail him with anything solid until now. Just by disappearing, he looks guilty, but now they have a witness with documented meeting dates and times. He's been working hand in hand with their gang and with a group of Syrian terrorists located somewhere in Georgia. And he's who ordered your kidnapping, but something tells me he had orders from someone else."

"Wait, back up. Syrians?" Jade interrupted, not sure if she'd heard correctly.

His mouth pulled into a thin line. "Not only is Celan greedy, but his moral compass is seriously fu...screwed up. He's been smuggling cocaine and was trying to import VX gas to a group of Syrians. He's got to know that shit is going to be used on Americans."

Jade swallowed hard as she tried to wrap her mind around everything David told her, but it was as if invisible steel bands had wrapped around her chest. VX gas? Syrians? Drugs in Saint Augustine? What was going on with the world? "I thought that woman was on the run from an abusive ex-husband. Never in a million years could I have guessed this."

"I know, honey," he said softly, although he didn't move from his seat at the kitchen table.

For that, she was thankful. She needed space to think, and he must have understood. Sometimes she thought he knew her better than herself. "So, what does any of this have to do with the ring?"

"The DEA is still trying to figure that out. The woman who gave it to you is with the DEA, but no one knows where she is, or if she's even alive. Since you were the last person so see her, and she gave it to you, they think it might be of some importance. While you were sleeping, I put it in my safe. Colin will send someone over to pick it up, probably tonight or early tomorrow morning."

"So what do we do now?" She twisted her hands in front of her.

"For now, you're under my protection. At least until this mess is straightened out."

"What about work or clothing? I don't have anything to wear."

"Colin has already talked to Maya, and someone will escort her to your place to pick up clothes and whatever else you might need. And work is out of the question. You're not going out in public until this guy is caught. Maya should actually be here soon so at least you'll be able to change."

Jade glanced at the wall clock, even though she already knew it was close to nine since all she'd done was stare at it for the past half hour. "You're not going to be charged with shooting the man at my store are you?"

David shook his head. "No, it was an obvious case of self-defense."

"I don't know if I ever thanked you for saving my life, David."

He shrugged, but fresh worry lines creased his face.

She took a step closer to where he sat and placed a light hand on his shoulder. "Don't act like it was no big deal. What you did was amazing and I should have thanked you before. If you hadn't been there…"

She didn't know how to go on. She hadn't seen much violence in her life, but she knew what would have happened if David hadn't been there. It was unthinkable. A sudden shiver racked her body, but it had nothing to do with being cold.

David pulled her into his lap and wrapped his arm around her waist. "But I was there, so don't think about what could have happened. No one is going to hurt you now, or ever again. I promise."

"I know." And she did. It was weird to think about, but David had always been her protector in so many ways, right from the beginning. After the death of her husband, he'd protected her from her well-meaning, but overbearing family, and from that moment, a bond had been forged. She might have been blind to his attraction, but he'd always been there, even as a friend. He'd wanted more, but he'd stood by and waited until she was ready. That knowledge alone warmed her heart in ways that almost left her speechless.

"David, I—"

The doorbell chimed and they both sighed.

Jade tried to push up, but David groaned and pulled her tighter against him. "Ignore it," he murmured into her ear.

She lightly pushed against his chest and chuckled at his resistance. "Come on, that's probably Maya."

He sighed heavily but didn't let her go. "Not so fast."

Before she knew what he planned, he brushed his lips against hers, softly at first, then more demanding. Deeper, hotter, than before, almost a sign of what was to come. A moan escaped her lips as his hands plunged into her hair, cradling her head. His teeth tugged her bottom lip and she let out a small gasp. This could get out of hand too quickly. She didn't want to but she pulled back, though she didn't say anything. She couldn't. She could barely breathe, let alone talk.

CHAPTER THIRTEEN

D avid grabbed the duffel bag and small rolling piece of luggage Maya had dropped in the foyer. He waited until Jade and her sister were out of sight before following up the stairs. Being too close to her was going to kill him. He knew she wanted him, that much was obvious. Every time she looked at him, desire flared in her emerald eyes. And surprise usually followed in equal measures. Why was she surprised by her attraction? He still didn't know what to make of that. She wanted him physically, but was that all?

His hands shook as he placed her bags in the guest room. This was the second time in his adult life his hands had ever wavered. Earlier that morning was the first. David's gut roiled as the image of that knife pressed against Jade's neck played in his head. He never should have let her out of his sight. She'd needed her space and to feel in control of things so he'd tried to give her that. The irony that he was in the business of protecting people wasn't lost on him.

He surveyed his guest room with disgust. She deserved better than this. The queen-sized bed, a crappy lamp, and a cheap walnut cherry nightstand were the only pieces of furniture in the sparse room. He'd never expected her to stay over, except in his fantasies. And in those, she'd been in his bedroom anyway.

Barely ten minutes later, he heard the front door shut, then not long after that, the sound of running water coming from the guest bathroom. After resetting his alarm system and securing the rest of the house, he took a shower and fell into bed. He wanted to talk to Jade—he wanted to do more than talk—but she needed to come to him. For this to go any further, she had to make the first move.

* * *

Jade let the scorching water rush over her body, unwilling to move from underneath the jets that pummeled her aching muscles. Her hair was washed, legs and other important areas shaved, and yet she didn't want to move. All she wanted to do was close her eyes and block out the world. Well, that and jump into David's bed.

Oh, how she wanted to do that. Especially after the most recent kiss they'd shared. What was stopping her? Her stupid inner voice, that's what. The stupid voice that screamed this could be a mistake. They'd done a lot of things but having sex would be crossing an invisible line. If things didn't work out between them she'd lose the best friend she'd ever had. Something she'd been taking for granted until recently.

She pressed her forehead against the cold tile and groaned aloud. She'd lose him anyway. He'd never go back to being friends, and if she was honest, she couldn't go back either. Too many things had changed. For both of them. His admission had rocked everything in her nice, tidy world on its axis. Barely a week ago she'd made the decision to start dating, and now she couldn't imagine anyone other than David touching or kissing her. Before that she hadn't been able to imagine *anyone* touching her. Now it was only David.

As she shut off the shower she knew she'd have to make the first move tonight. And she needed to figure out what she was going to wear. After toweling off and drying her hair, she stalked to the bed and unzipped her suitcase and pulled out what her sister had packed.

In one hand, she held the red satin and lace halter-style lingerie that screamed 'take me now'. The see-through wispy bit of material left nothing to the imagination. In the other hand, she held a black, cotton cami and boyshort pajama set. Still sexy, but not as obvious. In the end, she chose the latter. Actually walking down the hall to David's bedroom in the red vixen getup took more guts than she had at the moment.

Before she could change her mind, she threw on the safer pajama set—which stopped just short of showing her butt cheeks—and proceeded down the hallway to David's room. A dim, bluish light shone under the doorway so she knocked. Softly. She couldn't even hear the sound of her fist on the door, probably because the blood rushing in her ears drowned out everything.

Seconds later the door swung open, and David stood in front of her wearing a pair of pinstriped blue and red boxer shorts. And nothing else. His chest somehow seemed broader tonight. God, he looked good enough to eat. She let out an audible gasp and had to remind herself to breathe. With willpower she didn't know she possessed, she tore her gaze from the top band of his boxers and focused on his face.

"Is everything okay? I've already reset the alarm in case you're worried." His caring expression nearly melted her.

She cleared her throat and took a tentative step forward. She didn't want to have this conversation in his hallway. She was already embarrassed enough. "No, it's not that. We didn't get a chance to talk after Maya left and…uh, can I come in?"

"Of course." With a curious expression, he stepped back and shut the door behind them.

The click resounded in her ears like a gong, and the finality of her decision hit her. This was going to happen, and she'd never wanted anything more in her life. She clasped her shaking hands in front of her and took in the rest of his room. Funny, she'd never been in here before, but it struck her as very fitting for his personality. This was definitely his haven.

"I've never been in your room before," she said, surveying her surroundings. A Bombay-style chest with a golden rich chestnut finish sat in one corner, and on top of it, an exotic rectangular lamp put off a romantic amber glow. An antique armoire with a similar finish faced his king-sized bed. The main centerpiece of the room was, of course, his bed.

His huge king-sized bed.

Her gaze lingered on the rumpled burgundy and gold bedding and she swallowed. Hard.

Realization dawned on David's sculpted face as his gaze trailed the length of her body. No doubt he was taking in her attire. "What are you doing here, Jade?"

She hated that he asked. Did he need her to spell it out for him? Okay, maybe he did. If she'd worn the red outfit and jumped him as soon as he'd opened the door he would have had no questions. Her inner voice mocked her with that knowledge.

"I want..." her voice trailed off and she was grateful the soft lighting hid the blush she felt sweeping across her cheeks and down her neck.

"What do you want?" Though spoken softly, his words still somehow came out as a guttural growl. He sounded fierce. Like a warrior.

"I want you. I want this." Much to her annoyance her voice shook. She wasn't second-guessing herself, she was just turned on and a little nervous.

He didn't say anything, just inched closer, like a hunter stalking his prey. A shiver ran down her spine at the gleam in his dark eyes. "Are you sure?"

She nodded, and even though tremors still raced through her body, her voice was firm and clear this time when she answered. "I've never been more positive about anything in my life, David. I want you to make love to me."

Those simple words unleashed an animal. His mouth descended on hers but not with the same restraint he'd demonstrated so far. This was a different side to him. Animalistic. Primitive.

One hand reached into her hair and gripped her head. The other snaked around her and grabbed onto her behind. He clutched onto her and dug his fingers into her partially exposed skin. That rock hard erection pressed against her stomach with insistency. She instinctively arched her body closer to his. A groan of pleasure escaped when his hands slid underneath her camisole.

He began teasing her nipples, pinching and palming them in little circles. So many things ran through her head at once, but she knew her life was about to change. She and David were no longer just friends.

"Too much clothing," she mumbled.

David pulled his head back and his mouth curled into a slow, sexy smile. Her thighs trembled at that look. "I think I can do something about that." His expression froze into one of horror. "Shit."

"What? What's wrong?" He didn't want to stop did he?

"I meant to get them...I can't believe it but...*shit*, I don't have any condoms." He muttered another colorful curse and raked a hand through his dark hair.

She stared at him for a long moment. "I'm on birth control. I had some problems with eating after...and anyway, my doctor put me on the pill so..."

He still didn't move. Just stared at her with an unreadable expression. Finally he spoke. "I'm clean, Jade. I was tested about eight months ago. I haven't been with anyone in longer than, well, it doesn't matter. I'm clean but this is a big choice."

"I want you inside me with no barriers." And she did. Considering the big step they were taking in their relationship she didn't want anything between them.

"You're sure?" His voice was hoarse.

Not trusting her voice, she nodded.

His mouth slanted over hers and his hands returned to what they'd been doing. A shiver ran through her as inch by inch he peeled the flimsy camisole over her head. As he did, he left a trail of moist kisses covering

198 | SAVANNAH STUART

her bare stomach, breasts, shoulders, neck, and finally the sensitive spot behind her ear.

His warm lips pressed against that spot and she wanted to crawl out of her skin when he scraped his teeth against her. The man seemed to know exactly what she liked. As if he knew her body better than she did.

After a few moments he pulled back, his breathing just as ragged as hers. Any earlier worries of panic at being naked in front of David completely disappeared when she saw the look on his face.

He swallowed hard, and unparalleled pleasure shot through her veins as his appreciative, almost worshipful gaze swept over her bare breasts. Without even touching her it was as if he'd softly caressed her. No man had ever looked at her the way David was.

Ever.

Not even...No. She wouldn't allow herself to go there. Tonight was only about them. Her and David.

For the most part, she knew men liked what they saw when they looked at her, but there was another word for the gleam in David's eyes. He must have been guarding himself for years because now he wasn't hiding his desire from her. His entire body was still for a long moment as he stared down at her. She wasn't even sure if he was breathing. She could see the vein in his neck pumping and in the dim light his dark eyes threatened to swallow her whole. She didn't move though, despite her desire to cover up. Standing in front of him so exposed she felt suddenly vulnerable.

Her nipples peaked into almost painful points as she waited for him to do something.

"Perfect. You're perfect," he murmured. He pulled her toward the bed, shucking his boxers as they moved. She barely had a moment to admire him before he'd pulled off her boyshort bottoms.

Then it was skin on skin.

David's taut, muscular skin against hers.

The light smattering of hair on his chest rubbed against her breasts, teasing her nipples, and she shivered at the erotic sensation. She'd never imagined the right- ness of it all. Being with David like this caused her to wonder why she'd waited so long.

For some reason she'd always thought he'd be a breast man, but when he stretched his body on top of hers and widened her legs with one of his thighs, she knew she'd been wrong. No, David would be the type of man to pay attention to *everything*.

A hot ache grew inside her as he trailed kisses down her body until he finally lowered his head between her legs. First, he licked and kissed her inner thighs, almost torturously, before centering on the most sensitive spot between her folds.

Her hips almost bucked off the bed as the gentle, rhythmic massage of his tongue sent sensual currents shooting from head to toe. Her fingers intertwined in his dark hair and she gripped his head the closer she came to climaxing. She hadn't expected it to happen so fast though she probably should have.

He'd already pleasured her this way—that felt like a lifetime ago—and now was no different. David would get her off at least once before he sank deep inside her. Somehow she knew that's what he was doing.

When he flicked against her clit again, her thighs clenched and her breathing came in shallow gasps. She moved her hips against him, and just when her body was ready to find release, he pulled his head back.

She started to protest when he captured one of her swollen nipples between his teeth. He tugged and teased with no mercy. The ache between her legs grew, but before she could dwell on it, one of his hands slid down her stomach and took over right where his tongue had just massacred her senseless.

One finger, then two slipped inside, and he started working her. In and out.

His thumb worked her clit, and his fingers gently worked their magic. At first, the pressure was a light massage, but when she started moving her hips, he stroked with more urgency. Almost immediately, her inner muscles contracted uncontrollably.

Trying to ground herself she grasped onto his shoulders and squeezed. Her tight sheath milked his fingers and her body practically begged for him to fill her completely. Despite the climax curling through her, she wanted more of him.

Felt positively greedy with the need.

She moaned his name as she came. She couldn't help it. "David" tore from her lips like a prayer.

"Say it again," he murmured against her cheek as he positioned himself at her wet, heated entrance.

She tried to clear the cobwebs from her brain. At this point, she was unsure of what her first name was. "Say what?"

"My name," he growled. "I want to hear *my* name on your lips." His dark eyes devoured every inch of her face, as if he could read her inner thoughts.

"David," she murmured over and over, as he pushed the tip of his penis inside her. As if intentionally trying to torture her, he pushed in only a fraction.

Her inner walls clenched tightly, wishing he filled her completely. But he didn't make a move. Not right away.

Instead he held his position, teasing both her nipples until they were swollen and ultra sensitive underneath his fingers. "Tell me what you want." He gently tugged on her earlobe as he rubbed his length against her slit.

Still refusing to penetrate her.

"I want you inside me," she rasped.

David pushed the head of his penis in, slowly at first, but when she opened her legs wider and moved her hips to meet his, he thrust hard. She let out a tiny cry, and he momentarily stilled. She was wet with her own juices and after her orgasm more than ready, but he was still big and it had been a while for her.

Her inner walls flexed around him as she adjusted to his size. When she pushed out a shaky breath she realized she'd been holding it. As she did, the tiny bit of tension inside her fell away.

He must have sensed it because he gripped her hips and began thrusting. Like an erotic, familiar dance, she grinded her body in tune with his. She almost felt possessed. Hungry with the need to give him as much pleasure as he'd given her.

Jade was so incredibly tight he knew their first time wouldn't be as long as he liked. That was why he'd made sure she came before he slid fully into her tight sheath. The second he'd done that he'd known game over was coming fast.

It was as if a current of pure heat had run up his spine when he entered her. That's what she made him feel. Electrified and hot.

Her soft hands moved around to his backside, gripping and pulling, as if she couldn't get close enough to him. Her eyes might be closed, but the ecstasy that played across her features filled him with pure, male satisfaction.

He'd put that look there.

He'd given her that pleasure.

No one but him.

She writhed underneath him, her eyes half closed and he drank in the sight of her movements, trying to memorize every inch of her petite, lean form. Golden brown hair pillowed around her face onto the satiny, sheets. Her perfect, small breasts rubbed against him. With each thrust the hard peaks teased his chest.

As she arched her body again, he inhaled her scent. Vanilla and jasmine surrounded him, pulling him deeper into the tangle that was pure Jade.

Sweet, willing Jade.

He wasn't going to last long the way things were going. He was *inside* her. That thought alone almost caused him to come on the spot. He knew it wasn't a dream because dreams didn't feel this good. No matter what it took he was going to keep that pleasure etched onto her face.

His. She was all his and would be from this moment on. Slight tremors shook his entire body as he restrained himself from coming just a bit longer.

He moved his hips against her while caressing her swollen, pink nipples with his fingers and mouth. He couldn't get enough of kissing and touching her. Now that she'd allowed him access to her body he wanted to caress every inch of her. Barely audible moans escaped from her every time he tugged or even touched her breasts. She was so sensitive everywhere it amazed him.

He resisted the urge to pound into her the way he wanted to. Their first time she had to feel safe with him, had to know that he had some semblance of self-control. Which he hoped he did. When she'd said she was on the Pill, he'd nearly lost control. It had taken everything in him to give her the foreplay she deserved when all he wanted to do was pound into her for hours.

But it had been a long time for her and he knew she'd be sore no matter what. Hell, it had been a long time for him too. Now he wished it hadn't been quite as long because he felt like a sex-starved prisoner allowed a conjugal visit for the first time in years.

Her legs tightened around his waist, but he loosened his grip on her hips, afraid he'd bruise her. His stomach muscles clenched when she lightly ran her nails down his back again and gripped his ass.

Silently she urged him deeper, harder. She didn't have to say a word but he knew what she wanted.

She was close to climaxing. Again. A vivid flush of color had risen over her breasts, neck, and her cheeks were tinged bright pink. Her breathing came in more shallow gasps, and her vagina was making quick, successive contractions. Jade tightened her arms and legs around him, and she searched out his mouth.

Hungrily and savagely, she kissed him, bit and tugged his bottom lip. With a sudden jolt her entire body shook. In astonishment, he watched as her eyes closed and involuntary tremors shook her body again.

Her slick, tight channel clenched around him tighter and tighter, milking him until he almost hurt. Even wet and turned on, she was tight. He kissed and lightly bit her neck as she climaxed. The scent of their sex rolled over him, driving him over the edge.

As her orgasm surged through her, he let go of his restraint. He buried his face in the pillow of her hair, and nipped at the most sensitive spot behind her ear just as she came down from her high.

His thrusts were wild and unsteady.

Just as quickly as she'd come, he did too. He finally yielded to the searing need that had been building within his body and soul for years. His body melted into hers, and the more moans that escaped her mouth, the more his own passion grew until the hot tide that raged through him exploded.

A kaleidoscope of colors flashed in front of him. He emptied himself inside her in long, hot jets of semen until he thrust one last time before collapsing on top.

He could have stayed that way forever. If she hadn't chuckled and pushed at his chest he might have don't just that.

He rolled to the side but pulled her with him so that she lay curled up against him. Neither one said a word. The only audible sounds were the whistling of the wind against the window panes and their erratic breathing. Round one might be over, but this was the beginning of a long night. Now that he'd had a full taste of her, he needed more.

His thoughts were affirmed when Jade propped herself up on one elbow and flashed him a seductive grin. "I hope you don't plan on getting much sleep tonight."

Hours later, Jade slept soundly, like a woman completely loved and sated, but David could only stare at the ceiling as shadows danced around the room. Her petite, lean body curled perfectly against his, exactly where she belonged. Despite the hard-on that wouldn't go away, he couldn't remember the last time he'd felt such peace. For years, he'd dreamed and fantasized about what sleeping with Jade would be like. What it would be like to sink deep inside her.

Nothing came close to the reality. Nothing.

Being with her, he finally felt like he belonged somewhere. Like he had a home.

Home. That was a novel idea. He'd left his alcoholic parents house at the age of eighteen, although he'd never considered that home. Not once. In the Navy, he'd traveled so much, and when he did get a chance to take leave he'd gone home with Aidan. Buying a house in Saint Augustine was the closest he'd ever come to putting down roots, but in the back of his head he'd never known if he would stay permanently. Now he had no doubts. Jade would never move away from her family, and he wouldn't live anywhere she wasn't.

* * *

David couldn't stop from grinning as he whisked eggs together in a plastic mixing bowl. He and Jade had made love three times since last night and then this morning so he knew Jade had to be starving. He'd had a piece of fruit while she was still sleeping, but she'd only had a couple sips of coffee before pouncing on him. Again. He wanted breakfast on the table by the time she came down from her shower.

For all his past fantasies, he'd never imagined that Jade would be a sex starved vixen. Hell, he could barely remember his fantasies now that he'd had the reality.

She was his now, although she might not realize to what extent. He was never letting her go. Now that they'd crossed that line, it was only a matter of time before he put a ring on her finger. Every man in a hundred mile radius would know she was taken.

"What are you grinning about?" Jade's voice startled him.

He looked up to see her standing a couple of feet from him, leaning against the fridge with an amused expression on her pretty face. Shock rippled through him. He hadn't even heard her come down the stairs. Further proof that being near her had short circuited his brain.

"You," he answered as he drank in the sight of her.

She wore a snug zip-up hoodie with a pink guitar plastered across the front and a pair of loose cotton drawstring pants that hung low on her hips, giving him a nice view of her taut stomach.

"Nice sweatshirt."

She rolled her eyes. "Don't even start. I used to wear this all the time in college. I can't imagine where Maya dredged this up from, but it's comfortable."

He raked another gaze over her. He didn't care what she wore. The less the better.

She moved closer and nudged him out of the way with her hip. "I hope you made extra because I could eat my own hand right now."

"If you'll pour us both something to drink, this will be ready in a few minutes."

"No problem."

The circumstances might suck, but having her under the same roof all the time was something he could definitely get used to. Way too easily. "Colin called while you were in the shower. He's sending someone over to pick up the ring. He would have done it last night but it sounds like things got crazy down at the station."

She shuddered. "Good, I'll be glad to have it out of my sight. It's done nothing but cause me trouble."

"Maybe." He placed a few strips of bacon into the frying pan.

"What do you mean maybe? I've almost been killed twice because of that thing," Jade muttered without looking up from pouring milk into one of the glasses.

"Yes, but it might have taken me much longer to seduce you if you hadn't been forced to share a roof with me."

Her cheeks flushed pink but she didn't respond.

As they both sat at the table, David found it hard to concentrate on his food. Every bite she took, she made little appreciative sounds similar to those she'd made only hours before. Instead of enjoying his eggs and bacon, all he could do was fight another hard-on. God, he should be sated after the night—and morning—they'd had, not ready to jump into bed again.

"Did Colin say when I'd be able to go home again?" she asked, interrupting his thoughts.

He shook his head and tried to clear the image of her naked body from his brain. "No, he thinks that until this situation is under control you need to be under constant protection. Even if he didn't, I do."

"I understand that, but I can't stay here indefinitely. Don't get me wrong, I'm not complaining about the company." She grinned as she took another bite of her breakfast.

"You could move in permanently, and I wouldn't mind." The comment was meant to be flippant, but as soon as the words were out of his mouth he knew he'd made a mistake.

Jade's green eyes widened. "Permanently?"

Did she have to look so horrified at the thought? He shrugged and managed to swallow a bite of his food before answering. "You know how I feel about you, Jade. I don't know what you want me to say."

"You can't be serious though. You really wouldn't care if I moved in tomorrow?"

"No." Why bother denying the truth when they both already knew the answer? He wanted her in his home and in his bed all the time. He wanted a ring on her finger so every man in the entire fucking state knew she was his.

She cleared her throat but wouldn't meet his gaze.

"Whatever it is, just come out and say it." His heart twisted that this revelation was that big of a deal. So what if he wanted to live with her? He'd already told her as much.

She brushed a loose strand of hair out of her face. "I don't...I'm not...I'm not ready for that kind of step. Last night was *amazing*, but..."

Something inside of him snapped. He knew he was overreacting but was powerless to stop the stupid words from escaping his mouth. "But what? You just want a fuck buddy until something better comes along?"

She gasped, and a knife sank into his gut at the visible flash of pain in her emerald eyes. "No, of course that's not—"

"I know that's not what you meant." Some days it nearly killed him how much he loved her, and to hear uncertainty in her voice after the night they'd shared was too much. He didn't want to listen to her say what a great friend he was or how much he meant to her. Not after last night.

He abruptly stood. "Look, I need to return some emails and check in with my partner, so if you need me I'll be in my office. I know I don't need to say it, but don't go anywhere, I still haven't heard from Colin."

"David, I..."

He stood in the doorway with his back to her, waiting in vain for her to continue. But she didn't. So he left.

What more was there to say anyway? He couldn't beg her to love him. If she didn't, she didn't. He'd just have to deal with it.

David took the stairs two at a time and resisted the urge to slam his office door, but only because Jade would think his anger was directed toward her. He was pissed at the situation but also at himself for acting like an ass-hole. The wounded look in her eyes when he'd accused her of wanting a fuck buddy tore at his heart.

He'd come to terms with his feelings for her but he knew this was all new for her. Hell, she'd just decided to start dating a few days ago. She hadn't even had sex in two years, and he was asking her...hell, what had he been asking?

He started to head back downstairs when Colin Called. He answered his phone on the first ring. "Tell me you have good news."

Colin grunted. "Depends on your definition. Just got a call that Celan has been seen in your area. If we catch him today, this could all be over for her."

David allowed himself to breathe a little easier as he went to find Jade. It wasn't great news, but something was better than nothing at all. He rounded the corner to the kitchen and the bottom of his world fell out.

"Shit." Beads of sweat rolled down his back despite the cool temperature.

"What is it? Talk to me man," Colin said.

He tried to answer but couldn't. A vise clamped around his chest. The red light on his alarm system that should have been blinking was off. Short of someone firing an RPG through a window, his house was nearly impenetrable from the outside. A fortress. But only if the alarm system that'd put him back nearly ten grand was on.

And it wasn't.

Since it couldn't have been disarmed from the outside, Jade must have done it herself.

He sprinted to the window and tried to tell himself this was just a mistake, that Jade was in her bedroom and he'd forgotten to set the alarm. He knew it wasn't true.

When he looked through the window, a low ringing started in his ears. He blinked once to make sure that what he was seeing was real. A man not much taller than Jade was pressing a nine millimeter to the back of her temple. The man looked around wildly so David stepped back into the shadows of his kitchen and forced himself to breathe. His first instinct was to rush outside, but he knew that would mean certain death for both of them.

Colin's voice brought him back down to earth. "What the fuck is going on, David?"

He kept his voice low. "Celan has Jade."

"Repeat that?"

"He's got her. No time to explain, but I think I know where he's taking her. Call your guy out front and tell him to back off. I don't want Celan getting spooked. Get backup over to her house but no sirens. Your men need to be so invisible that I can't see them, and make sure they know I'm coming. If anything happens to her..."

He didn't finish. He didn't need to.

CHAPTER FOURTEEN

Ten minutes earlier

Jade pushed away her half-full plate and tried to swallow the lump in her throat. She'd never seen David hurt before, and the look in his eyes clawed at her insides. Angry and possessive she could deal with, but hurting him made her ache. She'd do anything to take back her words and erase that almost tangible pain she'd witnessed. What had she been trying to say anyway? His mention of living together had startled her, but only because of guilt. Not because it scared her.

After cleaning up the kitchen, she grabbed the full trash bag and went out the back door. David's trashcans were on the side of his house and helping him clean was the least she could do. She tossed the bag in but froze at the sound of a familiar male voice behind her.

"Do as I say and you'll probably get through this alive."

"I'm supposed to trust the man who sent people to kill me?" She was unable to disguise the tremor in her voice.

"I don't give a shit if you trust me or not. Turn around. Now."

Jade did as he asked and when she turned around, she wasn't surprised. The missing DEA agent, Keith Celan stood in front of her pointing a gun directly at her chest. And his hands weren't shaking. Other than the sheen of sweat across his pasty forehead, he looked like he did this kind of thing every day. Although it did appear as if he'd slept in his suit for the past few days. "What do you want from me?"

"I want you to move," he said.

When she stood there his face reddened.

"Move! Don't make me say it again." He motioned toward the side of the house with his gun.

God, where was David? She should have told him she was going out to the deck. She thought she'd only be a few seconds. He probably thought she was in her room.

"What do you want from me?" At least her voice wasn't shaky anymore.

"What do you think? I want that ring you said you sold."

She started to protest but then thought better of it. When he spoke again she was thankful she didn't try to deny it.

"Good girl, if you lie to me again, I won't be so forgiving." She felt the muzzle of his gun push deeper into her spine, and her blood turned to ice.

She wasn't sure how he knew she'd lied to him, but it was obvious he had no doubts. They continued to follow the stone path, but he pulled her to a stop just as they were about to round the corner of the house.

"Don't make a sound." He walked up next to her and moved the gun to the side of her temple as he peered around the corner of the house.

She swallowed hard and fought the chill threatening to overtake her. She couldn't afford to start shaking uncontrollably and have him freak out and shoot her. She wasn't sure what he was doing until she saw a Chevy Impala cruising down the street at an unusually slow speed. No doubt an unmarked police car. Before she could think of a way to get his attention, Keith shoved her behind a bush and hunkered down beside her.

"They've been driving by all morning. I'm lucky you were stupid enough to be outside," he muttered in disgust.

As soon as the car was out of sight, he yanked her to her feet and shoved her in the direction of David's next door neighbor's house, a raised, Caribbean style villa. She tried to scan the neighborhood for any signs of life, but no one was around. When they stopped underneath a semi-hidden open garage directly below the house, he shoved her toward the four door sedan.

"Get in the car." His voice was clipped.

"No." The word came out strong and clear, though she sounded much braver than she actually felt.

His eyes narrowed dangerously. "I don't think you understand. I'm not asking, I'm telling. Get in the car or I shoot you right here, right now."

"Fine, shoot me. I'm not going anywhere until you tell me where you're taking me."

He chambered a round and for an instant Jade thought he actually would shoot her. Everything around her funneled out, and all she could focus on was his bloodshot eyes. Finally he spoke. "I just want that fucking ring Evelyn gave to you. Once I get it, you're free to go."

He couldn't be in his right mind if he thought she still had the ring. But Colin hadn't mentioned it in her original police report so maybe he thought she hadn't told anyone about it. *Keep him talking.* That's the only thing that would help her survive this. "How do I know you won't kill me once I've given it to you?"

"You don't. But I'll kill your boyfriend right now if you don't tell me where that ring is."

Despite the chill in the air, she wiped sweaty palms against her pants. She couldn't let anything happen to David. "Boyfriend?"

"Don't play stupid. I've seen you two together a couple times. Do you really want to put your lover's life in danger? Do what I say and no one has to get hurt."

She couldn't put David's life in danger. She'd already lost one man she loved to violence, and she refused to lose David, not now. There was only one possible choice. "It's at my house." The words tumbled out before she had a chance to think about what she was saying. When they got there he'd know she was lying but she needed to get him away from David.

He eyed her for a moment, then motioned again to the vehicle with his gun. "You drive. If you try anything I'll blow your fucking head off."

She had no doubt that he would. The dead space in his eyes guaranteed he'd make good on his promise. There were no keys in the ignition so she waited for him. He got in the back seat behind her and dangled the jagged pieces of metal in her face. With darkly tinted windows, it was unlikely that David would recognize her even if he was outside.

As she reversed into the driveway she tried to keep him talking. "How did you get the keys to this vehicle?" She spared a quick glance in the rearview mirror. He was staring out the window, but at least he acknowledged her.

"There was an extra set of keys in their utility room. It's part of the house, but the alarm system isn't connected to that room. Idiots," he muttered.

She breathed a sigh of relief. At least he hadn't done anything to the family. She didn't know them, but she'd seen a mother with two little girls on regular occasions playing in the front yard.

"Why do you want this ring so much?"

"What are we, friends? It's going to be a whole lot better for you if you just keep your mouth shut. If you'd cooperated earlier you'd never be in this mess." He slumped against the seat.

She risked another glance at him through the rear-view mirror. He looked ready to keel over at any moment. Taking his advice, she kept quiet but couldn't stop the pounding of her heart. Once they got to her house, he was going to know she'd lied, then he'd kill her for sure. The drive was a short one and growing shorter by the second. In less than five minutes, she could be dead and the only regret she had was she didn't get to tell David how much she loved him. And not just as a friend.

How pathetic that it took a gun being shoved in her face for her to realize it. He'd been her rock for so many years, one of the main constants in her life, waiting until she was ready before making his move. She might not be ready to move in with him, but she knew she loved him. On some level, she'd known longer than she cared to admit. He was her best friend and now her lover. If it had been physically possible, she'd have kicked herself.

"Turn here." Keith's voice interrupted her thoughts.

"What? Why?" They were still a block away from her street. He had to know where she lived considering he'd sent someone to break in.

"There's a uniform posted outside the front of your house so we're going in the back way. Park there." He pointed toward the curb in front of one of the empty historical homes.

As soon as Jade's feet touched the cobblestone street, Keith grabbed the keys from her hand and shoved the gun into her ribcage. Instinctively she started to struggle but relaxed and followed his lead as they crossed the street. The street they were on paralleled hers. This time of day most people were already at work, so the chances of anyone seeing her was slim. Even if someone did spot them, nothing looked out of the ordinary. It's not as if he was flailing his gun around, and considering she usually jogged in the area, her presence wasn't out of place.

"We cut through here," he said.

He increased his speed, forcing her to follow suit, as they cut across someone's lawn. As they inched down the side of the house his breathing became more erratic.

"Open it." He wiped away the dripping sweat from his forehead and gestured toward the latch of the wooden privacy fence.

She did as she was instructed, and after a quick scan of the backyard, they darted across the lawn into the cover of some orange trees.

"Now what?" The privacy fence was close to seven feet tall. Did he expect them to jump it?

"Now we climb." Apparently he did.

"Don't get any smart ideas. We climb together, and if you even look like you're about to run, I put a bullet in that pretty face of yours."

She swallowed hard and nodded, trying to give the appearance that she was terrified. Which she was but that didn't mean she wasn't going to risk trying to escape. She had no choice. If she let him in her house there was only one outcome.

They both started scaling the fence at the same time, using the horizontal beams for foot support.

"All right, we go over at the same time." He balanced the gun in his right hand while trying to hold on to the top of the fence.

As she started to swing her left leg over, Keith faltered. This might be her only chance. Since she was slightly higher on the fence than he was, she struck out with her foot, knocking him in the head and forcing him off balance. The gun dropped from his hand. In slow motion, she watched the gun fall into the dirt on the same side of the fence.

"You stupid bitch," he snarled and dropped from his holding position.

For a split second she contemplated taking him on physically for the gun but opted against it. With strength she didn't know she possessed, she propelled herself over the fence and landed on her shoulder. Pain splintered through her body, but she was beyond caring. A loud pop sounded, and wood splintered all over her back. She clawed at the dirt, forcing herself to her feet.

He wouldn't miss again. Ignoring the throbbing pain in her arm, she sprinted across her backyard. She lost her one of her flip-flops and stumbled, nearly crashing to the ground again. The thought of a bullet in her back propelled her onward. If she could just get inside, she might have a chance to escape.

Jade risked a quick glance behind her and saw Keith drop from the fence to the grass, gun in hand. Their eyes met for a brief moment and she had a clear understanding what trapped animals must feel like. He'd made it over the fence faster than she'd hoped and now she wouldn't have a chance to get her hide-a-key.

He raised the gun in her direction. She dove behind one of the oak trees. Dirt and grass shot up barely a foot from her hiding place.

She unzipped her sweatshirt and threw it to the right of the tree, then ran left toward the corner of the house. Not a great distraction, but it was all she had and the tree gave her some cover. If she could just get through the fence bordering her home, she'd be free. He'd said there was a cop watching her house. All she needed to do was get to her front yard.

Blood rushed in her ears, and she couldn't stop her hands from shaking. She unfastened the latch on the fence and shoved it open. She jerked to a momentary halt, but gained back her momentum. David was crouched by the wall, gun in hand. He held out his hand and she started to move toward him, but there was a loud popping sound. Then a foreign, tingling sensation in her back forced her to her knees.

As quickly as it had come, the tingling turned to a burning, raging, ripping pain. She felt as if someone had taken a baseball bat to her back. David jumped up from his position and in a blur sprinted past. She tried to turn around. She needed to warn him that Keith had a gun, but the only thing she could manage to do was curl up on the grass. Staccato pops sounded all around her.

A warm, sticky liquid trickled down her neck and onto her face. She cringed. Blood. Blood was all over her face. She tried to instruct her hand to wipe it away, but her body wasn't listening to her. Tears distorted her vision as reality sank in.

She'd been shot.

David might be lying hurt or dead in her backyard, and she couldn't do a thing to help him.

In the distance, she thought she heard the faint sound of sirens but didn't know if it was her imagination. She attempted to lift her head again when strong hands lifted her off the ground.

David's voice shook. She thought she saw tears in his eyes but couldn't be sure because her own eyes were so blurry. "Talk to me, Jade. Say something, anything."

I'm here, I'm alive, her brain screamed, but no words came.

Through a haze, she watched David choke back a sob. Desperate to comfort him, she managed to clutch onto his T-shirt. His eyes widened, and as if through a tunnel she heard him shouting orders at someone like a drill sergeant. Whatever was going on, she knew he'd take care of her. He always took care of her. Now that she knew he was safe, she let the blackness she'd been fighting engulf her.

* * *

Jade opened her eyes to unfamiliar surroundings but it didn't take long to figure out where she was. Her arm was hooked up to an IV, and stark white walls and matching white furniture surrounded her. The smell of antiseptic and death was unmistakable. She glanced around, trying to find a call button when the door whooshed open.

"Hi." A pretty, petite, and familiar looking woman stood at the foot of her bed, wringing her hands nervously.

"What, uh..." Jade stopped, unsure of what to say to the woman who had caused her so much trouble.

"I'm Evelyn. I know you must have a lot of questions. I'd love to stay and fill you in, but unfortunately I can't. I waited until you came out of surgery..."

Everything was so fuzzy. Images of her parents and men in masks hovering over her flashed randomly. "Surgery?"

Evelyn nodded, her dark ponytail bouncing around her head. "You were shot once in the back. The bullet was close to the spine, and they had to do surgery immediately. You're lucky to be alive."

Jade's stomach clenched. "David. Is he all right?"

"He's down in the cafeteria with your family getting coffee. Listen, I'm sorry I can't stay and explain everything to you, and I don't know if I'll ever be able to truly repay you, but thank you."

Jade shook her head slightly, ignoring the pain that splintered through her skull. "I didn't do anything."

Evelyn smiled. "Yes, you did. David told me how you refused to give my ring to that bastard Keith. You saved my life and probably thousands of American lives."

"I don't understand." Lord, even talking hurt her head.

"I know, but I promise your boyfriend will explain everything to you."

Almost on cue, the door swung open and David stepped into the room. Before she could protest the woman ducked out and David was by her bedside holding one of her hands. Dark circles ringed under his eyes.

She managed a small smile and held her other hand out to grasp his. She gripped it so tightly, she was afraid she'd draw blood, but she couldn't find it in her to care. She needed to know he was real, that he was alive. "I'm so sorry, David."

"What could you possibly be sorry for?" His voice was hoarse.

"I don't know, for being an idiot and going outside without protection. How about for almost getting you killed?" She struggled to sit up, but with gentle hands, he pushed her back down.

"Jade, it's over. I don't give a shit about any of that. The only thing I care about is that you're alive. I've only got a few minutes before your family comes barging in, so let me get this out. I don't care how much time it takes for you to come around because I know we're supposed to be together. I was being an asshole expecting you to have all the answers right now. If anything, I should be begging your forgiveness, not the other way—"

"I love you. I've loved you for longer than I've been able to admit to even myself. You're my best friend, and when I was being held hostage, the only thing I could think of was that I had to survive so I could tell you just how much you mean to me and how much I can't wait to spend the rest of our lives together."

His response was a deep, lingering kiss. Jade thought she heard the sound of the door open, but if anyone had come in, they didn't stick around long. Minutes later, with much restraint, she pulled away. "I don't want to start something I can't finish.

"Good point." He still held her hand tightly.

Jade leaned back against her pillow. "What exactly happened?"

Luckily, David gave her a very condensed version.

Twenty minutes later, her headache was worse but at least the pain meds had started to kick in again. "Let me get this straight, Evelyn thought her boss had sold her out, and that's why she was in hiding?"

David nodded. "Apparently so. Only one person knew about her undercover status, and that was her boss. What she didn't know was that he purposely let her position slip to Celan in an attempt to flush him out. Before he could warn her, she'd been ambushed and assumed the worst. She did the only she could and went into hiding."

"You still haven't explained what the ring had to do with anything." Jade's head hurt, her entire body ached, and all she really wanted to do was sleep, but she needed to hear the rest of the story first.

David shook his head and grinned. Jade's stomach clenched at the softening of his features. "The top of the ring is actually a hinged lid and opens up to reveal a tiny hidden compartment. She wasn't sure what was going to happen to her so she placed a microchip in it with information explaining who she was, and pictures and proof of what she'd been doing. She also listed the coordinates of where she'd hidden a stash of the VX gas. It was a shot in the dark, but it was all she had until she could figure out who she could trust."

"Why not go to the media?"

David shook his head. "I asked the same thing, and she said that if it was her boss like she originally believed, he would have been able to sweep everything under the rug. She had to have solid proof he was a traitor before she turned to any authorities because otherwise it was her word against his."

Jade rubbed her temple and tried to absorb all that had happened in the past couple weeks. "It's hard to believe that a few weeks ago I was telling Maya that I wanted a little excitement and some hot sex in my life, and now I have both."

"You told her you wanted hot sex, huh?" His deep voice was unsteady and that dark, promising look she was coming to love was back.

She nodded and pulled him closer. "Yes, and you've more than fulfilled my expectations."

"I hope you're not tired of me just yet." He dropped a sensuous kiss on her lips.

"I plan to keep you around for the next forty of fifty years." And she did. She'd been given a second chance at love and she planned to take it.

EPILOGUE

Six months later

"That's the last of it. The guys are gone but said they'd be over Friday for the barbeque," David said, striding into the kitchen he now shared with Jade. "And, I'm just a blip on your radar now, aren't I?"

She looked up from where she was diving into the platter of cupcakes her mom had left earlier that morning and grinned. "Can you blame me? These are ridiculous. Want one?"

He shook his head as he crossed the short distance to her. "I don't want to lose a hand," he murmured teasingly.

She swiped off a bit of the icing and held it out to his lips. "You're the only man I'd share these with."

When he sucked her finger into his mouth, her eyes went heavy-lidded as she watched it disappear.

Setting down the cupcake she pulled her finger out of his mouth and wrapped her arms around his neck. "Are you nervous?" Her sweet scent wrapped around him, making him a little crazy.

"About?"

"Moving in here?" He, Colin, and a few other guys had moved most of his stuff into her—their—place, finally finishing a few minutes ago. Unpacking would take a while, but he was essentially moved in. Hell, he'd been over here almost every night since she'd been released from the hospital so it wasn't that big of a change.

They'd talked about moving into his house, but hers was central to downtown and he knew she loved it. His place had just been somewhere he'd slept at night. Home was wherever Jade was. He snorted at her question. "What do you think?"

"I think it's too late to back out now. I'm not letting you go." Pulling him closer, she stood up on tiptoe.

Bending to brush his lips over hers, he tightened his grip around her and automatically deepened their kiss, sinking into her sweet taste. He wasn't letting her go either. And tonight he planned to make it official. Moving in was one thing, but he wanted a ring on her finger, wanted her to take his name and have his children. And he was ready whenever she was.

He wanted everything from this smart, beautiful woman and wasn't sure he was going to be able to wait even the next few hours to give her the engagement ring that had been burning a hole in his pocket for the last couple months. "Good because I'm not going anywhere."

Thank you for reading Tempting Target. I really hope you enjoyed both stories and that you'll consider leaving a review at one of your favorite online retailers. It's a great way to help other readers discover new books. I appreciate all reviews.

If you don't want to miss any future releases, please feel free to join my newsletter. I only send out a newsletter for new releases or sales news. Please find the signup link on my website:
http://www.savannahstuartauthor.com

ABOUT THE AUTHOR

Savannah Stuart is the pseudonym of *New York Times* and *USA Today* bestselling author Katie Reus. Under this name she writes slightly hotter romance than her mainstream books. Her stories still have a touch of intrigue, suspense, or the paranormal and the one thing she always includes is a happy ending. She lives in the South with her very own real life hero. In addition to writing (and reading of course!) she loves traveling with her husband.

For more information about Savannah's books please visit her website at: www.savannahstuartauthor.com.

Made in the USA
Lexington, KY
12 August 2019